Who's Next?

Who's Next?

BOOK 2 OF THE HARP SERIES

D.E. Hopper

Deeds Publishing | Athens

Published by Deeds Publishing in Athens, GA
www.deedspublishing.com

Printed in The United States of America

Cover design by Mark Babcock.

ISBN 978-1-950794-33-1

Books are available in quantity for promotional or premium use. For information, email info@deedspublishing.com.

First Edition, 2020

10 9 8 7 6 5 4 3 2 1

I dedicate this book to my wife, Mary Stephens Hopper, for her unflagging support and encouragement during the difficult processes of writing and publishing.

1

He had escaped death and a murder charge with only one more bullet wound, a big pile of money, and a new outlook on life. Though he had escaped death many times in a long military career, and been wounded many times, he had never before come away with a big pile of money. Life was good.

Totally recovered from the most recent wound to an already mangled right leg, retired SMSgt. Horace B. "Harp" Harper happily strolled to his beloved Battle Bar with only the slightest limp. It was a beautiful spring day in Trenton, New Jersey. He had jogged three miles, massaged the shot up, shrapnel-lacerated leg, read another few chapters in a new book, cursed the news, showered, and donned his well-worn khakis and plain cotton shirt. He was feeling that all was right with the world. He was looking forward to the quiet dimness of his favorite bar's interior and his first sip of its finest bourbon. He could afford it now and was determined to savor every damned drop every damned day.

On this day, as in previous days, it appeared at first that nothing had changed at the Battle. It was the same as it had been since his run-in with the rogue Feds and near fatal cross-country flight about two years ago. But, something had changed at the

Battle. The bartender, the same short, bald guy with shiny face and scarred eyebrows who had been there for years, seemed unusually attentive. He was wearing his usual striped shirt rolled up at the sleeves, a worn bowtie, and an apron doubled and tied at the waist. He had, from Harp's first appearance at the Battle, sensed Harp's desire for privacy and left him alone on his stool at the end of the bar. But, today, he would walk up to where Harp was sitting, pause, and then walk away.

He could be forgiven for hesitating. Frankly, Harp had the look which discouraged small talk. In fact, it discouraged any talk—and Harp liked it that way. His face was tanned and lined, with a big nose between cool gray eyes, strong jaw, wide mouth, unshaven cheeks, and a mop of curly hair way behind on haircuts. There was a long lateral scar under his lower lip and dime-sized hunk of cartilage blown out of his right ear. He had a face that was not built for smiles and a forehead with a built-in frown. He just naturally looked like a man in a bad mood. People like this, you leave alone.

Finally, having made up his mind, the bartender waited for Harp to motion for another drink and then brought his idea along with the bourbon. He poured it, put it on the bar, and, this time, stayed. "Can I ask you somethin'?" he finally said.

Harp was surprised at this break from routine but knew the guy was working up to something. "Sure."

"You like this place, right?" The bartender's gaze was direct and intense. He was a small guy, maybe five-six, but there was not an ounce of fear in his eyes.

"Yeah, I do like it. Why?"

"Why is because we gotta shut it down pretty soon if we don't get a buyer." Harp could see the guy was really on edge.

"I didn't know it was for sale." He knew businesses across the city were shutting down over taxes, fees, license requirements, and employee problems, but the Battle seemed impervious.

"The guy that owned the place died and his widow, God bless that woman, wants to unload the building, the bar, the business, everything." The bartender rubbed his face with both hands. "An' she don't care about the help, the customers, the history, nothing." He put both hands showing scarred knuckles on the drink rail and added. "An' she says if it ain't sold by the end of next month, she's going to shut it down."

"What's that got to do with me?" Harp asked. "Apart from having to find another watering hole?"

"It's got to do with the stuff you drink." There was a slight triumphant note to his voice.

Harp could not see the connection. "How's that?"

"Anybody that comes into this place most every day and sits and drinks five six seven shots at fifteen bucks per has got to have money." Harp could see his logic. He was right.

"An' I was wonderin' maybe cause you like the place, you got the money, maybe you would like to buy it," the bartender concluded his pitch with a hopeful note. He seemed embarrassed with his own desperation.

The many thoughts jostling for the front of Harp's brain at this moment confused this experienced warrior who was used to making instant life and death decisions on the run. The sensible thoughts that would quickly eliminate an idea like this quickly bounced to the front. They were: permanence, responsibility, and people. That is, being nice to people. He was not very good at being nice to people. Hell, he was not nice to anything, including dogs, neighbors, and salesmen. Further, the mere thought of new responsibilities was a stab to his brain. But, those fact-based thoughts were pushed aside by two secondary, but much more appealing thoughts: free drinks—and every man's dream of one day owning a bar. Naturally it was those secondary thoughts that compelled him to ask the fateful question that would change his life forever. "What's she want for it?"

"You can have it all for half a mil asking but you might get it for less. That includes the whole building, the bar, the license, and, if you buy it, it includes me and the morning people." He waved his arm around to encompass the whole room. "We'll stay with the place. We're happy here and make a decent living off wages and tips. So, you got a good staff which, I gotta tell you, ain't easy to find."

Harp knew he should not ask one damned question. He should get up and leave immediately. Alarms were going off in the back of his mind. His mouth opened anyway and spoke. "What the hell are morning people?"

"They're the ones who open, clean, stock the coolers, and serve till I come in at three. There's two of them who come in to open. There's Johnny Dele and Lew Dunham. They open the place at eight. They do all the stocking and cleaning. Johnny also does all the empties in the basement—which, as I recall, you are quite famil-iar with." Harp winced at the memory of his escape through the basement long ago. Tommy noticed and let it go. He continued, "Johnny just works till about 10:45 and then leaves for another job. He's got family with kids to support. All he does is work. Lew tends the bar till I come in at three. I work the bar three to eleven an' sometimes close earlier. This is a working stiffs' bar and there's hardly anybody in here after ten. Plus, in this neighborhood, no-body wants to be out walking around after ten or so."

4

After this long statement, he thought some more. Then, he added, "We don't serve food anymore, so I can handle the bar by myself." He breathed noisily through a nose which had obviously been broken. "My name is Tommy, by the way. Tommy McArthur. I fought as "Tommy Two Fist" back in the day 'cause I could hit just as hard with either hand." He stuck his hand over the bar and Harp took it. It was like holding a small piece of warm granite.

"Harp," was all that Harp offered as he shook Tommy's hand. He was still very wary of the way this was progressing.

Now that he thought about it, Harp couldn't remember ever actually looking at the building from any distance. He remembered two stories and that was it. "What did you mean when you said 'the whole building'?"

"When you come in the front, what you see is just half of the stoop. That other half," he pointed behind Harp, "was closed off way back when and the downstairs over there was used as office space for some real estate guy, and there was a dance studio upstairs. You get upstairs over there by going straight in. You go right to get to the downstairs offices. It's all part of this same building." Tommy left to serve a beer to another patron. Harp was trying to digest all that Tommy had told him. He might, he just might, see himself owning a little bar but he sure as hell did not want to own an office building slash dance studio. The bartender returned and continued. "Manny, the guy who died and left it to Tawny, his widow, shut that side down after the last tenant left. That was four or five years ago."

"Tawny?" Harp had to ask.

"She was a stripper who worked as Tawny Tigress till her pasties started getting caught in the tassels on her G-string, if you know what I mean." Harp shuddered. He could only imagine. Tommy added, "But, Manny loved her and they were happy."

Tommy brought Harp another drink and went on describing the space next door. "About that dance studio upstairs, there was this woman, her name was Luna Norse. She seemed like a real nice young woman, late twenties maybe, who ran the studio for a couple of years, but all of a sudden she just up and disappeared." Tommy seemed mildly puzzled. "I been up there and she left everything like she was just coming back from lunch. Don't know what would cause that. I mean, hell, there was an old dried up cup of coffee on her desk, like she quit drinking it and went out the door. Pens, pencils, and notes like for students, you know? Just all layin' there."

Harp had to ask, "What's upstairs on this side then?"

"Nothing much up there now. Just a few pieces of old furniture they left 'cause they didn't want to pay to bring it down all those stairs. But it's mostly empty. It's a long hall down one side with four rooms off to the side. There's an old kitchen up there with nothing hooked up. It's got a dumbwaiter down to this kitchen. The main entry is that door outside there to the left of our front window." He jerked his thumb over his shoulder toward where the door would be outside. That door had never registered as part of this building. Tommy continued. "There's another narrow set of stairs behind a door in the downstairs kitchen. I guess so the owner or somebody could go up and down that way."

That was enough for one day, Harp thought. He felt like he should be running from this stupid idea. He wanted to finish his drinks and go home where he could give it some half-assed consideration and then forget it. For him, the very thought seemed almost laughable. He had to admit, though, that he really did not want the Battle to close. He liked the place. The location was perfect, just a block and a half from his apartment. Tommy was watching him as if he could see the thoughts going through Harp's mind. Money wasn't an issue. He still had a couple million left from the sale of that cursed Bardberg farm. When he got right down to it, the primary objection was that he did not want *any* responsibility at all right now. After those recent deadly months, he wanted to be left alone to finish recuperating in his current slow and well-oiled way. He left early. Harp paid for his drinks with a fairly new black credit card. It was the only one he carried. It was amazing how much credit you could get if you didn't need it.

"Let me think about it. Just don't bug me unless I ask, okay?" Tommy merely nodded at this rudeness and said nothing.

2

It nearly drove him nuts. Instead of *maybe* thinking about it, it was all he could think about. Harp concluded that he needed to know more—just out of curiosity, of course. There was a lawyer he knew who could advise him on just about anything relating to real estate. She was the one who put together that tricky farm sale that brought five million bucks to Harp and the crew who risked their lives for him. He gave them three and kept two. The trouble was, this lawyer might not be speaking to Harp at the moment. She suspected that he was the one who had somehow assassinated a very powerful person who had threatened her and her family. She was right. Harp nailed him on a golf course at about 600 yards. A great shot. And, Harp had gotten away with it. She was, however, not particularly appreciative of this manner of protecting her. She believed in the law. With a curious combination of apprehension and anticipation, he called her office.

Sandra Kowalski was one of Trenton's finest lawyers. During the period when Harp was dealing with that damned farm and his own life was on the line, she and Harp had shared a few very dangerous and passionate moments. The memories of those moments were so intense that they kept them apart rather than, as one would expect, bringing them together. Each felt there was not enough oxygen in the air when they were together. They had to stay apart just to breathe. Surprisingly, after a long wait on hold, Kowalski came on the line. "If this has anything to do with an inheritance, I do not want to talk to you. If this has anything to do with sex, I do not want to talk to you. If this has anything to do with death, drugs, or prison, I do not want to talk to you. Now, given that you may be smart enough to function within those parameters, what the hell do you want, Harper?"

Oddly, Harp was not a bit surprised at this. He expected it. He was actually standing there with eyes closed and smiling with what was probably the closest he would come to a look of tenderness. God, he loved this woman. "I am thinking of buying The Battle. I need advice."

"Goodbye, Harper." There was a click, then silence. Harp expected this. He waited, decided to try again, and redialed.

This time the secretary had a message and she read it as it had been dictated. "Miss Kowalski said, and I quote, 'I do not have time for a secretive, destructive, freaking, barfly killer who wants to play with his own damned saloon in a questionable part of the city.'" She was silent then continued reading. "She did say, however, that she would let one of our paralegals assist you. His name is Claude Leonard and he is very good at these things." There was a pause as paper rustled, "Oh, there was one more thing, Miss Kowalski said, 'Stay gone.' I'll connect you with Mr. Leonard." Harp now recognized the voice of this secretary. She was the one who had asked him the name of the dog Harp had adopted at that farm. That wonderful courageous dog's name was Fart. Fart was dead and now buried on a farm in North Carolina. Kowalski's office had a good laugh at his expense. For proof of his identity, the secretary asked for the dog's name. Harp stupidly gave it in one word. This secretary pretended that he was telling her what to do and was outraged. Kowalski thought it was very funny. Harp had been calling about a pile of bodies in a cave on his inherited farm. He didn't think that was funny.

3

Mr. Leonard was as good as claimed. It took only four days for the report to arrive via registered mail, and it was very detailed. *The property at 428 Magellan Street, Trenton, NJ, known as The Old Battle Bar consists of a single two-story building on lot no. 765J, Book 346, of 112ft. By 60.3ft., constructed in 1928 of brown brick on steel frame with external dimensions of 60 ft. in width by 77.5 ft. in length by 38.4 ft. in height exclusive of antenna structures with an internal space of 8,005 sq. ft., half up and half down. The condition is rated as good for current use with recent roof replacement and recent replacement of heat and AC units. The condition of interior plumbing and electrical services is unknown but suitable for passing inspections. Residential use is not allowed. The building fronts on a pedestrian sidewalk 12 ft. in width. It has a vehicular accessible shared alleyway in the rear. Rear upper doors access a joint fire escape with a drop-down ladder to the alley. Current use is a retail spirits (beer, liquor, wine.) establishment in the west half of the building (License No. 78956) with vacant office/studio on the east half. There are no liens or encumbrances against the property now owned by the estate of Manuel Obregata, deceased April 26, 2005. Appraised value in current use is $627,498. Current property taxes are $23,752* *per annum.* Attached was a bill for this service. Harp winced. The bill was for $809.00. He suspected that Kowalski had a role in arriving at this number.

In other words, the business was free and clear, available, and the building was in pretty good shape. It appeared to also be a good investment at the price quoted by Tommy. But it would be a management nightmare for an inexperienced, brash, troubled, angry, ex-soldier who badly needed more time free of any attachments until he had truly gotten his shit together. A really dumb idea. Really stupid. So, Harp decided that, if he could get it for the half mil, he would go ahead and buy it. The taxes seemed high but renting out the east side could easily pay for that. Oh boy, Harp realized, I am now thinking like a damned landlord and I don't even own the place yet.

In just a few weeks, he did own the place. Tawny accepted his offer of $485,000 cash, and the deal was quickly consummated, using her attorney for the closing. Senior Master Sergeant Horace B. "Harp" Harper, retired, became the owner of a retail liquor establishment on the edge of downtown Trenton, New Jersey. Far from the battlefield where he acquitted himself so admirably as to receive many medals for bravery and valor, he was now the suddenly frightened and unsure owner of the Old Battle Bar, commonly known as "The Battle."

But, in spite of his rough beginning as a child of the streets of Trenton, Harp's Army career had taught him the need to approach any duty and/or obligation with singular focus and application. He was thus determined to learn all aspects of the operation of this establishment of which he was suddenly the sole owner. Harp was there when it opened the day after the title closing. He watched the morning crew go through all the steps it took to open a bar for a new day. Johnny Dele and Lew Dunham knew he was the new owner and that he was watching. Dele was a quiet graduate student who went about his duties with a determined air. He wore the uniform of a cleaning service, which was the job he went to when he left the Battle. Harp couldn't imagine when he found time for school. Dunham was a tall, slumping local with prominent cheekbones, small eyes, and wide mouth. He was a local product, with parents living nearby. He barely graduated from high school. They self-consciously cleaned the floors and the bar, stocked the coolers, and cleaned the bathrooms. At times, all this was done while at the same time serving the few morning customers who, for the most part, were shaky individuals who needed a jolt to start their day. Harp had been drinking from a very young age, but he never needed a 100-proof hit to start the day. He was there when Tommy came at 2:30. He watched as Lew handed over the duties and Tommy checked the total in the cash register and reconciled the income and outgo prior to the transition to his shift.

During a slow time, mid-afternoon, Harp got the keys from Tommy and studied the rest of his new property. He first went up the inside stairs from the kitchen to the upstairs apartment. The huge front room was painted a depressing off-pink color and was twenty-seven feet wide and nearly as long with high tin ceilings. The extremely tall, elaborate, round-topped windows provided a harsh light that seemed designed to illuminate the coldness of this abandoned space. Even Harp shuddered when he looked around the room. The kitchen was bare, furnished with absolutely no modern appliance, just a sink and old tin cabinets. Harp turned one of the spigots on the sink and it didn't work. Two bedrooms were empty except for an ancient metal dresser in one. There was a functional iron fire escape at the back. Harp thought that living here would be a form of punishment.

He next visited the other half of the building next door with head-shaking wonder, thinking, *I don't want this. This is not me.* The former insurance office on the lower floor still held desks, chairs, file cabinets, and even a huge printer. The power was off. All the drawers were empty. Everything was coated with dust. There were blinds on the windows that remained fully closed. He opened them briefly and decided to leave them closed. This office took only two-thirds of the floor. There was a small bathroom with a commode, sink, and narrow metal shower stall. Beyond a clearly modern sheet rock wall, the last twenty feet held only empty cardboard boxes and some cleaning equipment. There was a locked door at the back opening to a dock with steps down to the alleyway.

He continued his tour, going out the insurance office door and up the stairs to the former dance studio. Again questioning his sanity, he was looking at an almost fully functional enterprise. The hardwood floor was still gleaming under the dust, and mirrors reached the length of the far wall, with one of those barres dancers used attached to the opposite wall. The small office area at the near end of the room was as Tommy described, with a calendar, papers, pens, and pencils all scattered across the top of the desk as if they would be taken up and used any minute. The drawers of the desk were still cluttered with the usual business junk. One drawer held a pair of those cloth shoes dancers wore and a small thing for holding up hair. Here, the same tall windows provided a different light, as if it had a purpose. There had been life in this room.

Harp came back down to the Battle with a confused mind.

All he wanted to do was own a bar. He did not want all the rest of this shit. Shaking it off, he decided that it was now time for a drink. Tommy brought it and started to ask a question. Harp closed his eyes and shook his head, still in a kind of shock. Tommy got it. He left Harp alone. Harp was still there at 10:35 when Tommy said, "Mr. Harper, we haven't had a customer in over a half hour. It's times like this when I usually decide to shut it down. Staying open any longer is just losin' money."

Harp had hardly said a thing all day. He just watched and learned. At Tommy's statement he said, "Makes sense." He watched as Tommy went to the front, locked the door, and turned off all the overhead lights and then the small open sign in the window. He watched as Tommy gathered the day's receipts and removed almost all the cash from the register and put it in a small canvas bag. Harp followed Tommy to the kitchen door in the far-right corner. Tommy unlocked the door and led Harp to a small cluttered, dusty office to the right in the corner of the kitchen. It had a small one-way mirrored window into the bar area. There was a good-sized safe against the wall.

Tommy gave Harp the combination. Harp opened the safe and put the bag in the safe. He closed it and opened it again just for practice. He then turned to Tommy and smiled. It had been a good day, and Harp was pleased at how well his property was being managed. Tommy beamed with pleasure and relief when Harp expressed his complete satisfaction. It meant that the Battle would stay open and Tommy could continue working.

Harp went home tired and worried. His mind was torn between two thoughts. One was: I'll be damned! This thing might work! I might actually be able to do this! The other was: I'm crazy! This is too much! There's no way I can make all this work!

4

It really wasn't Harp's fault that Dominic Donetti died on the sidewalk a couple doors down from the Battle a few weeks after Harp had taken ownership. If Dominic had done his homework, he would have known that you do not approach a battle-scarred, often ill-tempered, field-hardened veteran of many wars with mere threats of bodily harm. Either you attack or you stay the hell away. In this instance, an arrogant finger poke on a warrior's chest resulted in a fatality.

The whole thing began with two events. The first occurred when Harp had come in to his new business early and happened to be there one Monday morning around eleven when a guy walked in carrying a slightly bulging leather satchel. The morning bartender, Lew, without being asked, set a shot of Canadian Club and an envelope on the bar in front of the guy. The guy glanced at Harp with an indifferent look, tossed the shot, put the envelope in the satchel, and left.

"Hey, Lew, what the hell was that all about?" Harp asked.

Lew suddenly looked very uncomfortable. "Didn't Tommy tell you?"

"No. You tell me."

"You know. The protection. Everybody pays it." Lew shrugged.

"How much is it?" Harp asked. He was now very interested.

"It's a hundred a week. We pay on Monday."

"Where does the money come from?"

"We take $20 from the till five days and put it in an envelope for Monday."

"You understand that this is *my* money, don't you Lew?"

"I know, I know. But listen, Mr. Harper, you really, really don't want to mess with this. It just ain't worth it. They hold all the cards. So many things can go wrong if you fight it. And, believe me, you can't fight back." Lew was extremely earnest in his appeal. "Tommy probably didn't tell you 'cause he probably didn't even think about it, we been doing it so long. It's natural, you know." Lew shrugged, tucked his elbows in and turned his hands up.

Harp was extremely annoyed. First, that Tommy had failed to tell him and, second, that some local prick could come into *his* bar, shoot a free drink, and then pocket a hundred bucks of his money. However, he was realistic enough to understand that it was a small enough cost for maintaining neighborhood peace, at least until he understood the consequences of not paying. "Okay, we'll keep doing it for now. I'll talk to Tommy when he comes in." Lew gave a big sigh of relief and went back to work. He was happy to work at the Battle. He had learned very early in his life that people with no gifts will do best in situations with no challenges.

The second event was an idea of Tommy's daughter, Laurie. She was a graduating senior majoring in performing arts at The College of New Jersey. She was Tommy's only child and of course in total ownership of his heart. Tommy's wife had died of cancer long ago. Laurie lived at home to control expenses while in school. She had been working from the beginning and was mostly debt free. Because of fortunate scheduling, they spent mornings together during which she would tell Tommy of her challenges and accomplishments at school, and he would tell her about the previous day's activities at the Battle. She was a sweet girl who listened to her father's hard-earned advice over the years and, as a result, was much more level-headed than most young women of twenty-four. She also listened as her father described the new owner of the Battle. She was happy her father was going to be able to keep working at the Battle. He really enjoyed his job.

Tommy might have been a bit too enthusiastic, however, in his description of Harp's wealth. The way he put it, Harp had unlimited resources to bring to any new endeavor. From such promise, a new idea sprang from the mind of Laurie. She had known about the insurance offices and the dance studio in what was now Harp's building. She was a student of dance. She was about to graduate. Jobs were scarce. Suppose she and two of her fellow graduates opened a dance studio? It would take a lot of work and they would likely starve for the first couple of years but, in their youth, they could only see the upside of the whole idea. They were smart young women, and they developed a reasonable proposal. Tommy was, of course, ready to chip in.

Thus was Harp, on a day like any other day, as he strolled into the Battle, confronted by the confusing picture of three young, attractive, women leaping to their feet as he entered. Harp turned to Tommy in confusion. Each wore black tights topped with some kind of long baggy shirt and colorful sneakers. Each had her hair done in a bun at the back of her head. Each was slender and looked exceedingly healthy. They did not belong in the Battle. Harp suddenly felt like he was very old.

"Mr. Harper, this here is my daughter Laurie." He spoke with obvious pride. The petite redhead in the middle kind of glided forward and held out a tiny hand. She appeared to be very nervous. "And these are her classmates, Jane and Carol." They too glided forward with outstretched hands then glided back. "They got a business proposition for you."

Harp, thoroughly puzzled and, as always, annoyed when he was puzzled, scowled at Tommy.

"Okay, let's go sit and talk about it." They moved to one of the tables in front. Harp listened as they described their circumstances. They were all graduating in dance and they would all be looking for jobs. Right now there weren't that many jobs. One after another would excitedly leap into the conversation with fluttering gestures as they described their situation. The bottom line was that they were broke. Jane and Carol even had student loans to pay off. Harp was having a little trouble following these thought processes, which seemed to be presented in a different language by three mouths at once. Eventually, he understood. They had a dream and he was being asked to make it possible. They wanted to do something together, and that something was to open a dance studio. They wanted to reopen the dance studio in Harp's building.

Harp's first thought was not just no, but no godammit. He liked things the way they were. But they persisted. They offered a deal. If Harp would let them have the studio free for six months, they would totally clean, repaint, and redecorate it. They would dress up the stairwell and put new hardware in the bathrooms

19

and on the doors. They would pay for utilities. At the end of six months, they would begin to pay him whatever rent he felt was fair. Much as he hated to admit it, they had made a solid pitch, and he couldn't see how he could lose.

They had not finished their proposal, however. Carol's brother, Aaron, was currently a junior associate in a large law firm and was totally dissatisfied with his work there. He wanted to open his own office. He also had little money but would work the same deal as the girls. Plus, Carol added, Aaron would do most of Harp's legal work free. Aaron was in Poughkeepsie at the moment but had seen the Battle building and had authorized Carol to speak on his behalf. All that space, too, would be cleaned, painted, repaired, and rented, and Harp would get free legal advice in the bargain. Again, Harp could not see a downside as long as all this happened in *their* part of his building. He agreed to their proposals on the spot. The Battle had never seen nor heard such excited hopping and squealing. Harp just winced and backed away in confused guilt for watching their petite perfect bouncing bodies. He escaped to his favorite stool at the end of the bar and pointed at his bottle with just a little desperation. The dancers started to follow, but Tommy quickly shook his head and waved them away. Harp shook his head and said "Goddammit, Tommy, what the hell just happened?" Tommy just grinned. He knew what happens when his daughter attacks with an idea.

While Harp could not see a downside for these proposals, he could not have imagined the depth of the downside that they would bring about.

5

Later, Harp once again happened to be in the Battle when the weasel who collected the "protection" came for the money. He watched sourly as Lew handed over the envelope and poured the Club. The collector put the envelope in a small canvas bag and tossed the shot. Harp couldn't stand it. He stepped between him and the door. "That will be five dollars."

The collector's mouth fell open in disbelief. "You fuckin' kidding me? We don't pay for drinks in the places we protect. It's part of the deal."

"No, I am not fuckin' kidding you, asshole. You can take your shitty protection cash but you are not going to drink my liquor in my bar without paying!" Harp was now standing almost nose to nose with the guy. "Get it?"

It did not take long for the mob collector to understand that he was seriously over-matched with this guy. He raised both hands palms out and said, "Okay, okay. I get it." Then, as Harp backed up a step, said, "I see you got lots of improvement going on next door." He showed bad teeth in a sly grin. "I'll have to let the boss know about maybe we need to reconsider how much it costs to protect your place, being as how you got all this new

21

business going on." He threw a tenner on the bar, told Lew to keep the change, then swaggered out.

Lew was looking at the floor and shaking his head. He sighed, "Boss, I gotta tell you, you shoulda left him alone. You don't have no idea the shit they can drop on you."

"Lew, who is *they*?"

"I don't know for sure, but I think the mob which has got this part of the city is run by a mob boss named Arturo Donetti. They was two or three of the mob biggies, Russian, Italian, and one other back around 2010. After they had some real bloody fights over territories, they had peace talks and divided the city into divisions. The guy they call 'Arty Boots' got this part, I heard." Lew washed some glasses while Harp watched and continued. "I don't know, Boss, whether I want to stay on if you are going to fuck with these guys. I am seriously attached to breathing an' I can't stand the sight of my own blood."

When Harp saw that Lew was scared, he realized that maybe he had gone too far. "Look, Lew, don't quit. I'll go along with their graft just to keep the peace. I'll agree that everything is going just fine and there will be no reason for trouble. Okay?" Lew nodded glumly.

"Where the hell did the name Arty Boots come from?" Harp had to ask.

Lew looked over his shoulder as if someone were listening. He leaned on the bar, lowered his voice, and replied, "They say there's a whole bunch of guys with concrete boots out in the river into which Arty put there."

Harp thought, Jesus, what the hell have I gotten myself into?

6

Work in the dance studio and lawyer's office proceeded ahead of schedule. Harp watched and had enough sense to simply stay out of the way. The energy of the young ladies and the young lawyer seemed bottomless. They worked from daylight to dark and had both places looking bright and attractive way ahead of schedule. They would come into the Battle from time to time for refills on their soft drinks, which Harp had directed be provided free of charge. The studio was signing up the first dancers at the end of four and a half months, and the lawyer had clients coming even before he was finished painting. There was an attractive sign on the entry to that half of Harp's building that proudly invited patrons to enter the *Pas de Trois Dance Academy* or the offices of Aaron Weaver, Esq., Attorney at Law. Oddly, Harp felt a sense of pride when he saw this sign. He was strangely proud that he had actually contributed to the success of these kids. He really liked Weaver and thought he had the right qualities for success: he was smart, educated, and a hard worker. He avoided the girls because he never knew what to say when they were around.

Somebody else saw this sign and it wasn't pride that he felt. He felt that somebody was getting away with something in his territory. Arty Boots had given his son Dominic this part of the territory a couple of years ago but was still angry that he had screwed up this one business because he couldn't keep his pecker in his pants. There had been a thriving dance studio and realtor's offices. Dominic had pursued the owner of the studio, who was a beautiful woman, and he hadn't been able to control her the way a man is supposed to. She suddenly disappeared after being appropriately punished, so the son was confident that no one would ever know the truth of what they did to her.

The guy who ran the realty business was a smartass who decided to move to another part of the state after the second beating. So, no more protection money coming in from these people. After these episodes, and because his father knew Manny Obregata from the old days, they left the Battle alone and kept the protection at a hundred bucks a week. As long as the Battle was the only thing in the building.

But, business was business. Dominic felt it was time for a talk with this guy who bought the Battle. Sure, the guy had agreed to continue paying protection, but that was just for the bar. Now he had three businesses going again on this property. It was time for an adjustment. It was only fair. He felt certain that his father would agree now that Manny was dead. He badly wanted to impress his daddy.

First they sent Vinnie the Dunce, the fucking *lo zaccone*, to announce the new rate of $400 per week. Dominic felt this was a very reasonable and mature approach. Vinnie came back with the usual $100 and a request to transfer this location to another collector. The new owner, he said, had a way of looking at you, like one inch from your nose, while daring you to make a move. Vinnie wasn't used to being scared, but this guy acted like a fucking killer, Vinnie swore. Plus, he said with piteous outrage, the fucker made him pay for his drink. Vinnie was sent back to waiting tables at the mob's favorite restaurant in Hoboken. It was called The Ristorante Marina.

It was decided that they would try one more time with this reasonable approach. The messenger was Fingers Pucinetta, a large, experienced collector who was known for his ability and willingness to break small bones as an instrument of persuasion. He returned with the same $100 as the Dunce. He also had a dislocated arm. "I ain't never seen a guy move so fast," he said. He was moved to a job as bouncer at the mob's strip club near the pier. It was called the Steak and Strip.

7

They had, of course, been watching Harp and had a good idea of his schedule. He would usually arrive at the Battle around five in the afternoon and leave at eight or so. However, since he had bought the place, he stayed until closing on Sundays. Though open for those patrons who needed their libations regardless of the recognition of the Sabbath, the Battle usually closed early, around eight. Harp would then stroll back to his condo nearby. Dominic thought this would be the best time to have a talk with this guy Harper.

It had been an especially pleasant Sunday at the Battle. Harp had spent most of the time finishing the changes he had started in the little office. He was happy to note that he now had a neat desk, a new office chair, understandable file cabinets, an uncluttered bulletin board, and empty trash cans. And, he had done it all while sipping his favorite bourbon. He was really enjoying being a businessman. He could now go home, get pissed off at the news, shut it off, throw the remote, and read his next book. Life was good.

That changed shortly on this fateful Sunday evening after he left the Battle. While passing, he had just waved back at Aaron

Weaver who was doing catch-up work in his office when two well-dressed guys straightened from where they had been leaning against a large black vehicle with tinted windows. It was one of those civilian hummers some men bought in a fruitless attempt to enlarge their genitals. They stepped in front of Harp when he was still some distance away. It took Harp about one second to read the situation. He stopped and waited. They weren't showing any weapons, but the slight bulges under their arms were a giveaway. Harp said nothing. Finally, the one on the left spoke. He was a big guy wearing an expensive black leather jacket with a blue turtleneck sweater.

"Mr. Donetti would like to talk to you." His voice was strangely high. His name was Booge. Harp guessed it was past damage to the larynx. He studied the one on the right. That one seemed leaner and more thoughtful.

Harp appeared to be thinking. He said, "Sorry, I don't know any Dough-nutty—outside the local bakery."

The guy was startled at this flip reply. "It's Donetti, not Doughnutty." He was suddenly nervous at this exchange and kept glancing at the car. Harp noticed one of the back windows was down a couple of inches. They were not accustomed to a casual response to their threatening presence.

"Still don't know him." Harp took a step forward and, as expected, they reacted with a certain tenseness with which he was very familiar; slightly crouched, arms brought up, leaning forward slightly. Though not as obvious, Harp tensed also. He was getting ready to attack.

The leaner one spoke. His name was Whip. He had a thin face with prominent nose. He held his hand mid-chest in front of his suit jacket in the unmistakable gesture of an armed man.

"That really doesn't matter, Mr. Harper; he would like to talk to you. It is a business discussion which he feels is quite necessary."

Harp shrugged. He appeared relaxed but they could not know that he was already in danger mode. "I'm easy to find."

Booge said, "Yeah, we found you and he wants to talk to you *now*." He finally made the slightest gesture toward his armpit signaling how far they were willing to go. "Would you please get in the car *now*."

Harp shrugged again, "Not getting in any car. Sorry. Maybe Mr. Dough-nutty could come by my office sometime next week. I have some time on Wednesday."

At this statement, the rear door of the vehicle was suddenly thrown open, propelled by an anger that also propelled a third guy to jump down out of that door and stride quickly toward Harp. This was exactly the wrong thing to do on several levels, the main one being that he came between the target and shooters. He stopped within a foot of Harp's face. "Listen, asshole. The name is Donetti, and you will regret ever making fun of this distinguished family name. I know you think you are some kind of tough guy but, believe me, you ain't seen tough." Harp just listened and studied Donetti. He was average height, slender, black-haired, brown-eyed, and had an oddly wide mouth with small gaps between all his very white teeth. Harp supposed he would be found attractive by some women.

Donetti continued in the same outraged manner, right hand finger pointing and wagging, "I came here in a peaceful way. I was going to discuss the amount of insurance you should pay. I was going to say that $400 would cover it." He stepped back, hand on chin, as if considering, "Now, asshole, things are different." He moved closer again, "Now you are going to pay $600 and," he began poking Harp in the chest, "if we get any more shit from you, you will find out why you need protection."

Harp quietly said, "Don't do that."

Dominic Donetti had grown too accustomed to being protected. First as a boy, then as a young man, and now as the son of a mob boss. In the small world in which they functioned, no one would think of harming the son of the Don. "Oh, tough guy, huh? Don't do that, huh?" With that, he started poking Harp in the chest with *both* fingers. "How about this, asshole?"

Thus, it was with great shock and surprise that he now found himself with both wrists dislocated by a lightening twist out and up. At Harp's quick movement and Dominic's scream, his two soldiers quickly moved in to protect their boss. Harp spun Dominic around and pushed him into Whip as he was reaching under his jacket. Almost in the same motion, he knuckle spiked Booge in the throat. He staggered back with both hands to his throat, desperately trying to breathe. Dominic fell into Whip just as Whip was bringing up his small nine-millimeter automatic. His intent would have been to just cover Harp while they got Dominic back in the Hummer. However, the weapon was off safety and the idiot had his finger on the trigger. Dominic's bulk pushed the weapon back at Whip, causing Whip's finger to involuntarily contract. Because of the proximity to Dominic's chest, the pop of the gunshot was greatly muffled.

The bullet pierced the center of his heart, immediately stopping its function, then was probably stopped by the bone in Dominic's spine. Whip tried to hold Dominic up while desperately trying to make the previous few seconds just go away. He finally gave up and let Dominic fall to the sidewalk. He landed on his back and lay there with eyes open, staring at nothing.

Booge rasped, "Jesus Christ, Whip, look what you done! You killed the Boss's son! You're fucking dead, man! Dead!" With that, Booge grabbed Whip and pulled him toward the Hummer. He pushed the still stunned Whip into the front seat, ran around to the driver's seat, and they roared away in a cloud of diesel smoke.

They had forgotten Harp, still standing in the middle of the sidewalk. He was wondering why this shit always seemed to follow him. As he opened his eyes and straightened, Aaron Weaver was standing there. There were people gathering around the body. Weaver quickly whispered, "I got the whole thing on my phone."

Harp heard the sirens approaching. He pulled Weaver aside. "That's good, Aaron. I want you to make that copy for me on a jump drive and then I want you to forget you ever saw a thing. Erase it from your phone. You must never, ever, be associated with this shit. Do you hear me? If this video is ever needed, it's going to come from an anonymous source." Weaver nodded, unsure. Harp continued with a hard look and undeniable sincerity, "You did not see a thing. Don't ever testify to anything. Okay? Now, get out of here. *Don't be a witness!*" Harp's intensity was unmistakable. Aaron understood. These were some really bad actors. They did not forgive and forget. As it turned out, there were other recordings, enough to put it all together without Aaron's.

Harp and the growing crowd were soon confronted with police cars coming in from both directions. Blue lights and red lights were bouncing off buildings, windows, cars, and people in a small part of Trenton, which suddenly assumed almost a festive atmosphere. The center of all the attention had two parts about which everything turned; there was a body and there was

Harp. Fortunately, there were eye-witnesses who saw parts of what happened. When these parts were put together by the police, it made a complete picture. Generally speaking, Harp had been accosted by these three guys. They attacked Harp and, when Harp pushed one of them away, the attacker accidentally shot one of his own guys. Harp did not have a weapon, so the shot had to come from one of the other three. One witness said that it appeared that the skinny one shot the dead guy while they were kind of hugging. He said it hardly made any sound at all. One said it was like a hand slapping a feather pillow. Another said it was like a balloon popping in a closet.

8

Harp knew the drill. He waited. He sat on the steps of another closed business while all the statements were taken. There was one uniformed cop who was not-so-casually keeping an eye on Harp as they waited. They had erected a barrier around the body to keep bystanders from taking phone photos. Unfortunately, by the time it was up, there had already been many photos taken. The world with which Harp and many of his age and experience were sometimes purposely unfamiliar allowed these photos to be transmitted around the world in minutes. Literally. Sometimes for money. "Son of Mob Boss Killed in Trenton!" was the headline. The London Tribune probably got them at the same time as the National Enquirer—each before the Trenton Coroner's assistant came in from his anniversary celebration to begin the official examination of the remains. Dominic did not look particularly bad. When Whip had dropped him, he landed on his back on the sidewalk and appeared to be sleeping. His eyes were closed, but his mouth was open as if in amazement. Because the heart had immediately stopped, the wound had bled very little. The dislocated hands appeared to the untrained eye to be normal but perhaps only slightly turned inward.

Detective Sergeant Jay Carroll, who was lead on this case, finally got around to Harp. He strolled over while reading his notes and sank tiredly next to Harp. He was wearing a tired blue suit over a once white shirt with a poorly knitted knit tie. He had a receding hairline, a long face, and a full lower lip that folded out when he brought a menthol cigarette up to his mouth. After a long drag on the cigarette and without any preliminary statement, he read from his notes with little puffs of smoke on the syllables while exhaling, "We looked you up. What we got here is you, Horace B. Harper, an honorably discharged veteran of the United States Army who came back to Trenton upon his discharge carrying all kinds of medals for heroism in several different theaters. Thank you for your service. You recently purchased an establishment known as The Battle Bar, which establishment has been open for fifty-some years." He turned a page. Harp carefully listened. "About three years ago, you were involved in a series of incidents in a place called Bardberg, PA, as a result of which there were seemingly related fatalities. You were a person of interest but not charged as causality could not be determined."

Carroll inhaled a good portion of his menthol cigarette and continued while exhaling. "You seemed to have exited that series of incidents with a clean sheet and a great deal of money. Something involving oil, gas, and mineral rights, it says." With tilted head and raised eyebrows, he turned to Harp with the unspoken question. Harp remained expressionless. Carroll shrugged and continued. "So, today, or tonight, while seemingly walking on this street on your way home, you are somehow engaged with three guys who get out of a large, black Hummer. At the end of this engagement, one guy is dead and the other two crawl back into the Hummer and speed away." He put the cigarette out and concluded, "Why don't you tell me what happened—and don't leave anything out." He pointedly moved the small digital recorder on his notepad and ground another cigarette butt into the pavement.

Harp told the whole story of the day's events, leaving nothing out except Aaron's witness. He described the confrontation in detail, including the punch to Booge's throat and the dislocating of Dominic's wrists. Carroll's eyebrows rose at this point in the narrative. Harp described hearing the shot that killed Dominic and the words spoken by Booge immediately after. He told Carroll about the protection money he had been paying and the opening of the studio and office, which had brought about the threat of a weekly increase. He told him about sending two of the goons away with various injuries when they tried to collect the increase. Carroll just looked at the sidewalk and smoked more cigarettes while Harp was relating his memory of the events.

When Harp was finished, it was dark. The cop lights were still bouncing around the street. Carroll hit the off button on the recorder and tilted his head back with eyes closed. He looked like he was taking a nap. Then he started shaking his head. Finally, he spoke. "We got witnesses who say the same thing. You were set upon by three rough looking guys and you fought them off. In the process, one of these guys shoots another one of these guys. You're just standing there when the shot is fired. You are unarmed, not even a stick. They run off, leaving the dead guy here on the sidewalk. You very politely wait for the law to arrive. Next, the law will say you are in the clear. You walk. Our job is done. Big fuckin' woopee." Another cop walked over to say something. Carroll said, "Give us a minute, Pete." The cop walked off.

Carroll continued. Now he was almost whispering. He was leaning toward Harp's ear. "Now, Mr. Harper, here's what happened on this beautiful Sunday evening in the real world." His face was blinking blue and red from the cop car lights as he spoke with fierce intensity. Harp was listening with equal intensity. "The only begotten and much beloved son of mob boss Arturo "Arty Boots" Donetti, by name of Dominic Donetti, decides to take a personal hand in making one H.B. Harper cough up more dinero for Mr. Harper's growing business. Mr. Harper tells Dominic, and by virtue of their close relationship, Mr. Arturo Donetti, to fuck off. He ain't paying more." Carroll pauses, lights a cigarette. "Now here's the fun part: in the process of confronting Mr. Harper, young Dominic is killed. True, he is shot through the heart by one of his own men; however, and this is one huge however, in the eyes of the father, his death is caused by the actions of one Mr. H.B. Harper who pushed his son into the gun."

Harp started to say something, but Carroll held up a hand to cut him off and went on. "Your guilt in the eyes of the law is irrelevant here. You are guilty in the eyes of Arty Boots, and he will come after you and there is nothing any of us can do about it." Carroll shrugged, "Oh, we can give you a guard for a while. But, I guarantee you he will be pulled off for budget reasons if we try to go more than a few days."

The been-in-the-business-too-long cop noticed that Harp was now barely listening. He seemed instead to be thinking about something. To make the point a little clearer, he continued, "Maybe you don't get it, Harper. I got about two more years and I'll have my thirty. I got no wife and my idiot kids haven't spoken to me in years because I am of the oppressor class. As soon as I retire, I'm moving to a small cabin on a lake in the Poconos where I am going to fish and smoke and drink until either my lungs or liver quit. When that happens, I will eat my Glock and be worms before I'm sixty." Carroll lit another cigarette and stood up. Harp stood also. They stood face to face. "I tell you this to make a point. Even given all that, *my future at this moment is a lot brighter than yours.* See you at the inquest." He turned to walk away.

"Where is he, the one who's going to come after me?" Harp asked, stopping Carroll, who took a moment to process the question.

"Why?" the cop asked.

"I guess I'd just like to know the direction it's coming from." Harp responded.

"You'll never see it coming. The best thing you can do is disappear. The trouble is with these fuckers, everybody you know and care about might disappear too." He thought for a minute, then decided what the hell. "Arturo Donetti has a mansion north of Trenton. The house is totally walled in with gates and cameras and the whole property is patrolled. Plus, they say he has another hideout somewhere, but nobody knows where it is."

Carroll again started to walk away but stopped to offer one last observation. "It's small consolation, but I think you've got a little while at least. He knows we know what he's probably going to do. If he moved too fast, we would be all over him, and he does not like that kind of attention. No, when it happens, he is going to be far away, and he will express great shock and surprise that such an awful thing would happen in this city."

The tired policeman then walked back to his car and drove away. The body was long gone, and even the most dedicated observers had gone home. It was now close to midnight. Harp was too tired to concentrate on the warning Carroll had given. He went home and went to bed. He would consider how to prepare tomorrow.

9

Dominic's death had made the news. It reached the ears and eyes of too many people in Harp's past. As a result, he had many annoying calls expressing concern for his welfare. Some he welcomed, like the calls from Bonny, Weeks, and Kip. This trio of warriors, Sgt. Marion Bondurant, Corporal Phillip Weeks, and Private Wellington Kipling Finch-Smithers IV, had been with Harp through the recent dangerous ownership of that cursed farm in Bardberg, PA. Together they had fought off the sinister attempts of wealthy Pittsburg magnate Adam Willarde, who would stop at nothing to own the farm Harp had inherited from an unknown cousin. The late Willarde had known of oil reserves worth millions on Harp's land. This fantastic potential had gone undetected until found by studies he secretly commissioned.

As a result of their actions to resist Willarde, men had died, one as a collective action and others at the hands of Harp, using a unique skill learned in the Army. Harp and his men had come under some scrutiny for these actions but had escaped official sanctions. After the farm was sold for more than five million, Bonny and Weeks became owner-operators of a large row crop/beef cattle operation in North Carolina. It was bought with money given to them by Harp after the sale. Kip had gone home to stay with his once estranged parents while going through a series of operations needed to correct damage to his face from an enemy bullet in Iraq. Each member of this unique squad offered to come to Trenton to stay with Harp if he needed them. Harp was touched and enjoyed hearing from his former comrades in arms, but firmly declared that he was doing fine and they should go on with their new lives.

Another call was from Pittsburg Police Detective Joe Stephens, who had investigated Willarde's death by a strange projectile that had apparently been fired from far away. He had rightfully considered Harp a suspect but was unable to find critical evidence tying him to the homicide. It was one of the big failures in a long law enforcement career, and he resented it still. His call was not friendly. He reaffirmed his belief that Harp had killed Willarde and suggested that Dominic's death was probably Harp's fault. To Stephens' disappointment, Harp explained that he had already been cleared of any wrong-doing and suggested that Stephens talk to Detective J. Carroll. Stephens hung up.

Two weeks after Dominic's death, Harp was hiding in the Battle's little office from the crowd of new patrons who were there just to spot him and ask questions. Tommy came back to say that Harp had a visitor. Harp assumed it was one of the annoying post-action gawkers who were now filling the bar. He suggested that Tommy relay the message that he was busy and couldn't see anyone right now. Tommy shook his head and, rarely for him, contradicted Harp and said Harp would want to talk to this lady. With a big sigh, Harp gave the okay.

Stepping hesitantly into the kitchen to where Harp stood

by the office door waiting, was an attractive woman in her early thirties. She was tall, slender, with auburn hair brought back in a tight bun, which, while severe, was not unattractive. Her face had pleasant, even features with hazel eyes made larger and somehow more attractive by rimless eyeglass lens of mild prescription. Harp stepped forward and extended his hand in greeting. She responded by clenching her hands at her breast and backing away. She appeared frightened. Puzzled, Harp dropped his hand and asked in his own unintendedly blunt way, "What do you want?"

At this question, she turned to leave the kitchen, then stopped and squared her shoulders. She turned back. "Mr. Harper, you have no idea what it cost me to come here," she said while looking at Harp, then away. He waited. "I came only because I know this place, this kitchen, this office. And, I once had good memories here." She waved both hands, vaguely pointing in all directions. "If you were anyplace else, I would not have come."

Harp asked, more gently, "Would you like to come in and sit? I can get us something to drink."

She shuddered, "No I cannot go into that office with you. We can talk right here."

Harp replied, slightly impatient now, "You can talk all you want, but I have things to do here so," he shrugged and raised his hands palms up, "talk." He leaned on the door frame and waited.

She took a deep breath and began. "My name is Luna Norse. I ran the dance studio upstairs next door."

Harp nodded, glad to finally meet the mysterious woman who had suddenly abandoned that business.

Norse continued. "At the time, all of us in this building got along. It was very pleasant. Business wasn't booming exactly for any of us, but we all made a decent living." A cloud moved across her face. "Of course, we all knew about the so called 'protection' money, but Manny Obregata handled it, and we were pretty much left out of the actual payment process." She took a deep breath, removed her glasses, and rubbed her eyes. "Then, somehow, I came to the attention of Dominic Donetti. Personally. He started showing up at closing time and would be waiting outside when I left." She shook her head as if shaking free from a bad memory. "He was attractive and personable and expressed his admiration for anyone involved in the beauty of dance. He was persistent, and polite, and funny."

While engaged in these memories, she absently sat on a nearby metal kitchen stool. She leaned on the stainless-steel table and resumed. "I was aware of his familial connections, but I was younger and more daring then and found it perversely exciting." She noticed the suggestion of contempt on Harp's face at this description of the late Donetti. "I know. I know. It was foolish. But I began seeing him. We dated for three months. He was younger and full of energy, and we engaged in a whirlwind of exciting activities from here all the way to New York City. It was fun. Money was no object. We went to the ballet even. He showed me all of his family businesses. I saw things that I knew were on the shady side, but I just laughed at all of it. You can't imagine what that was like for a small-town girl from Indiana. It had not hit me yet that he was showing me all of the family operations because he was thinking of me as part of the family!"

Her face clouded again. She clenched her hands. "For me, it was all just fun. I had no thoughts of a permanent relationship. But, that's what he wanted, and I couldn't see it until it was too late. He assumed I felt the same way. Assuming this, he took me one Saturday to a place that he called the family's secret hide-away. He said it was for family only. It was a strange estate kind of in the middle of nowhere where the driveway was probably a mile long. He made a big deal out of introducing me to his father Arturo who was happy that his son was happy."

Norse started softly crying. Harp handed her a kitchen towel. After a deep breath, she resumed. "His father blessed our union and gave both of us big hugs and kisses on our cheeks. That's when it hit me! This was all about a proposal!" She laughed bitterly. "This small-town girl from Indiana was brought up to tell the truth, even when it hurts. I could have delayed it. I could have asked for time to think about it. But, no. I blurted out that I could not marry him because I didn't love him." Norse shook her head in wonder. "The change was remarkable. The cruelty and meanness came out immediately. He just asked if I was sure. I said yes. I could see the change come in stages," now whispering as she continued. "There was disbelief, then maybe some sadness, then rage, and then what I could only describe as madness. He hit me in the stomach, then again, then in the chest, then when I bent over, in the back, down low. I was in agony."

Norse looked at Harp with a sense of wonder. "Even in the midst of his rage, he was careful not to leave any visible marks. Who could do that?" she asked plaintively, slowly shaking her head. She then lowered her forehead to her arms crossed on the cold steel table. Harp sat quietly, totally absorbed in this recitation, waiting.

Without asking, Harp filled two glasses from the kitchen with water and placed one in front of Norse. She straightened and drank several swallows before resuming. "Thanks. They left me alone in a room, I think it was the guest bedroom, for an hour or so. Then Arturo came in. He said, 'So, you little whore, you think you're too good for my son, huh? Do you know what we do with whores?'"

She closed her eyes and spoke again after a long pause. "'We fuck them,' he said. 'We fuck them wherever and whenever we want to.'" Harp could tell that this was a woman who would never use that word. "And then he raped me. I was in so much pain, I couldn't fight him. Then Dominic came in and he raped me, calling me names the whole time. We got there on a Saturday. They took turns all evening and then all day Sunday."

She looked at Harp with fierceness in her eyes. "You will never understand what rape does. You become a hole, a socket, a receptacle into which things are pushed. Your humanness is gone. You don't have a heart or a brain or a past or a present! Your whole being is changed from a thinking, feeling, enjoying, creating person to a goddamned place to stick something!"

Harp was now shaking his head in disbelief. Norse was crying again. "They made me scrub myself in a shower. They made me flush myself out. They took me back to my apartment late Sunday night and told me that if I ever said anything about it to anyone, they would kill me and kill all my family. They said they would even kill my pets. They said they would kill my children if I ever had any."

She sat up and pointed around generally. "That's when I left here. I left everything. I threw some clothes in a suitcase and drove to Indiana. I told no one. I have been living in terror with this secret in a small town where everyone now thinks I am deranged. They look at me in pity and leave me alone. That has been my life: wondering if the next car on the street is them."

Harp was moved. His heart had gone out to this woman. "Why tell me now?" he gently asked.

She smiled for the first time. "Because of you, Dominic is dead. That part of the horror is over. I came here to thank you." Then she added, "But that's not all. I came to warn you. They will come after you. They won't forget, ever."

"Well, I appreciate that." Harp said, somewhat inadequately. "But I have already been warned."

Norse stood. She now looked Harp in the eye. "I am going back home tomorrow. I am going to try to resume a normal life. Maybe it's selfish, but I feel much better having spilled all this poison here in your business. I hate myself for saying it, but now maybe they will come after you and forget all about me. I'm sorry, but I thank you for listening." She concluded with intensity, "I prayed every day for their deaths. Now I need to pray for only one of them to die."

Harp stood also.

She wasn't finished. She leaned closer over the table. "There's more. I know where he is and I know where he hides all his money. Dominic had a tendency to brag. When he assumed I was joining the family, he told me things he wasn't supposed to. I listened and I remembered." She paused as she remembered. "I asked once if his father was really rich. He laughed. Then he said his father had a ton of money. I said, you mean he is really loaded. He laughed again, and said, no, I mean he has a ton of money. I said I didn't believe that. He said, well, you'll be sleeping on top of it tonight. I said I didn't understand anything he was saying. He said that his father was the secret banker holding all the cash for a lot of dirty businesses in this state. They all had so much paper money, they didn't know what to do with it, so his father started a kind of bank. He kept it all at this place in the mountains. It was somewhere under the bedroom where we were supposed to sleep. A ton of money."

Harp was intrigued but merely asked again, "Why are you telling me?"

Norse shrugged. She now seemed different. More relaxed. "Who else? They will come after you. Maybe if you know their secrets you might find a way to fight back. Someday, when you are ready, let me know. I want to help." Then she left.

10

By ten weeks after Dominic's death, the Battle had been ruined. Not ruined in a business sense, but ruined for Harp, Tommy, and the morning guys. It was no longer the way they wanted it. It had become an attraction. It was now a lively, successful *scene* making lots of money. It was an *in* place. There was laughter, noise, and demands for complex drinks and even food. Some nights, people stood two deep at the bar waiting for their drinks. Harp had to hire two new bartenders to help Tommy and Lew. And, perversely, it all happened because Dominic Donetti died a few feet away. The story had caught the public eye, and people starting showing up to see where it happened.

They wore designer jeans and Rolexes. This was the place that had refused to pay the mob protection. The mob guy died right out there. The chalk outline was drawn and re-drawn when it washed away. It was like a pilgrimage. They all had to first walk by the outline of Dominic's body where it fell. Of course, all this traffic brought more people past the signs for the dance studio and Weaver's law practice. They, too, experienced a huge increase in business. The difference was, they welcomed it. They were delighted. Harp was despondent. He had no place to go.

Harp found that if he was in the Battle when the evening crowd poured in, everybody wanted to shake the hand that killed Dominic Donetti. Though he felt a sense of duty to take care of things because he was the owner, he hated all of it. This was definitely not him. He wanted out.

Harp and Tommy secretly began looking for another bar that would be like the Battle used to be. Harp had approached Tommy with the idea and found him to be "totally fuckin' ready." They were determined to re-create that dark, quiet, neighborhood atmosphere. It had to be utterly devoid of cuteness and/or coolness. Basically, they were looking for a failed establishment. Tommy's contacts had found three prospects a few blocks away. One had been closed for years over health violations, one had lost its liquor license over big time sports betting, and the third had closed for seemingly no reason.

The first two were available for very reasonable prices but, when they visited these properties, the reasons became obvious. They were trashed. They had bad wiring, the plumbing had been leaking, and they had been stripped of anything worth a buck. They were basically filthy rooms emptied of everything but junk. The third establishment was not listed for sale. From what they could see very dimly through the windows, it might be just what they were looking for. It was a stand-alone two-story building similar in size to just the bar half of the Battle building. The name was a very unimaginative *Ed and Hal's*. There was a door in the middle with a line of chest-high windows to the right and left. It had its own parking lot to the left and a fenced in half lot to the right with small trees on each corner. They liked it. The trouble was, they could not find the owner to talk about it.

After a couple of visits just to look through the windows

and bang on the front door, Harp happened to pass by later one evening. He was on the other side of the street looking at the place when he noticed a faint light in the upstairs windows. He parked his SUV and walked over to the building. This time he walked around to the side and found a solid brown door with a small awning hidden behind the tree. There was a doorbell button and small speaker. Harp pushed the button.

"We don't need any," said a voice speaking loudly in the speaker after a few seconds. It was the voice of an elderly man.

Harp pushed the button again. "What the hell do you want? Go away."

And, pushing the button again and not waiting for an answer, Harp shouted into the speaker, "I want to buy your business."

"It's not for sale. Goodbye."

Again. "Can we talk about it at least? It's just what I've been looking for."

"Are you a goddamned real estate salesman?"

"No, I'm a regular citizen. I have one bar and I don't like to drink there anymore and I want to move to another one."

"You want to buy a bar so you will have a place to drink?" the voice said in disbelief.

Harp shrugged. He realized it was crazy. "Yes."

The speaker sounded after a long pause. "That's one of the dumbest things I have heard in a long time. You got cash money?"

"Yes."

"Go out and stand in the street where I can get a look at you." Harp stood in the middle of the street and looked up at the windows. The curtains moved in the middle one and closed. Harp walked back to the door and waited.

"You look pretty damned rough."

Harp replied, "The fact is, I *am* pretty damned rough. But I earned it." He was getting annoyed at the manner of this exchange and had decided to hell with it.

As he turned to leave, there was a buzz at the lock and the speaker said, "Come on up. It's unlocked. I have a gun, so don't try anything."

Harp took his time climbing the long flight of stairs. He was trying to imagine what he might encounter when he got to the top. It was another locked door. This one had a peephole, which darkened as he was studied from inside. The door was then opened by a man probably in his mid-eighties who stood back to let Harp pass into what was obviously the kitchen. He was holding a large ornate highly reticulated revolver in his right hand. He gestured toward a kitchen table and said, "Sit."

Harp could have taken the gun away from him, but he was really curious about what the hell was going on. So, he went to the table and sat. He watched as the old man closed the door and locked it. Harp thought he looked a lot like Andrew Jackson, with a long narrow face and white hair that stood high on top of his head. He might have been tall once but was now bent at the shoulder and knees. He was wearing baggy pants with suspenders, an old flannel shirt, and a cardigan sweater with frayed cuffs.

The old man went to the opposite side of the table and painfully sank onto a chair. He leaned on his left arm and waggled the sidearm while pointing it at the ceiling and asked, "Do you know what this is?" It was supposed to be a warning gesture, Harp knew, but it only served to emphasize the old man's age as the heavy weapon was held in a shaking hand.

Harp answered, "Yeah, it's a piece of shit Russian 7.62 Nagent gas-sealed 7-shot double-action revolver, which only an idiot would carry in battle. You had to kick out and load shells one by one. Probably made in the thirties. It was really heavy and required a big holster. I would be surprised if you had any ammo and I would really be surprised if it would fire any of the old stuff." He smiled at the look of surprise on the old man's face. Harp did not add that there were still idiots out there using these things. He had killed some of them.

The old man smiled and laid the pistol on the table. "Well, like most of these old things we brought home, they only have to work once." Before Harp could process that statement, he continued, "You want a drink?" He saw that Harp was about to decline and offered, "When we closed the bar, I kept a few bottles of the very best stuff. He slowly walked to a cabinet and pulled down a bottle of the oldest bourbon Harp had ever seen. Thirty years. It's presence on his tongue was a revelation. One way or another, Harp thought, I have got to find a case of this stuff.

For a quiet moment, they sat sipping and enjoying. Finally, the bar owner introduced himself, "My name is Edgar Priest. Me and my brother Hal owned this place. He died eight years ago. Cancer. Smoking. He didn't have anybody but me. I tried to run it by myself, but I didn't have the energy or drive anymore, so I closed it." He sipped his drink. "I have put off selling it because this is where I live and I didn't want all the noise and shit going on downstairs and I don't need the money now." Harp wondered what the "now" was about.

"What's your name?" Priest suddenly asked.

Harp replied, "H.B. Harper, I go by Harp to most people."

"You a veteran?"

"Yup. I'm retired after 24 years, kicked out on disability, and doing okay."

"Which war?" Priest gruffly asked.

"There were several." At any given time, the U.S. had troops in Afghanistan, Iraq, Libya, Syria, Niger, Yemen, and Somalia. Harp had only seen four of them. There was one other country not on this list where Harp served. That one single incursion brought a world of trouble down on his shoulders.

"Which one were you?" Harp asked, somehow assuming the guy was a veteran.

"Korean. That's where the Nagent comes from. Took it off an officer after I shot him." He smiled. "He was trying to load it."

Harp laughed. They both relaxed a little.

Priest continued in a quiet voice, looking over Harp's shoulder at some point far in his past, "I was there at Inchon in 1951, when we invaded North Korea. They pulled me out of my duty with occupation forces in Post War Japan." He sipped a little, smiled, "I was a snot-nosed kid and I went from real sweet duty to utter hell overnight. And I stayed in that hell for another two years." He looked sharply at Harp, "You seen pure hell?" Harp knew he was talking about the battlefield.

Harp replied simply, "Yup. Seen it. Done it."

Priest nodded as if confirming something in his mind. He struggled to his feet again. "You want to go down and look at the place? I don't want to turn on all the lights. It might give someone the idea we're open."

Harp nodded, "Sure."

Priest stood and walked toward the back of the building. "We'll go down the stairs back here. I had hand rails put in at the right level for me to go down the steps. My knees are about gone, and I am too damned old for replacements. Easy coming up but hard as hell going down."

Harp went first and descended slowly, keeping pace with Priest. As with the Battle, the stairs came out in the back of the kitchen. The room was dark, but Harp could tell that it was clean and orderly. They went through the kitchen and into the bar area. With a few changes, it was strikingly similar to the Battle. Harp made up his mind immediately but said nothing. Priest had dropped tiredly into a well-worn wooden chair while Harp studied the place in detail. He now had a better idea of what to look for in a business like this and took his time. Even in the dim light he could see that the place had been well managed. He marveled at the ancient and ornate wooden back bar with its shelves and mirrors. He didn't think it would take long for Tommy and him to set it up and get it going. It would mean a longer walk, but hell, he was still jogging several miles a week. A little extra walk wouldn't hurt. "I got cleaners coming in once a month to keep the dust down. The coolers have been empty for years, but I think they still work."

"You ready to talk about selling it?" Harp asked. They were both sitting in the dim light at a table along the wall near the bar. Just like the Battle. Both knew there was more to that question than the words conveyed.

Priest sat looking at Harp. He drummed his fingers on the table, then scratched his chin. He turned in his chair to look at the bar, at the front of the place, then the back. "Well, Mr. Harper, until you showed up, I didn't think I was ready. Now, sitting here, looking at what me and my brother had going once, knowing we are never going to do that again, I am ready." He then repeated himself, almost as if expressing a revelation. "I am ready." Then, with this new sense of discovery, "I think I've been ready for a while now." He shook his head and smiled sadly.

"You want to talk money now?" Harp asked.

"Yes and no. We need to have an understanding first."

Oh, hell, Harp thought. He knew this was going too well. "Okay, what about?"

"I will sell it to you and give you a serious discount if you will do something for me." He paused. "I want you to drive me to Rochester, New York."

"That's it?" Harp asked, surprised at the simplicity of the stipulation.

"Yes, that's it." Priest tapped the table as he gave details. "This property was last appraised at somewhere around $350,000. It would come out some less because it hasn't been open for a while. I will give it to you for $295,000 if you hurry to get all the legal stuff done for the sale and title transfer. When it's all done, I want you to hand me that money in cold hard cash, and then I want you to drive me to Rochester as soon as possible after the close."

Harp thought that didn't seem like much. He guessed it wouldn't take more than six or seven hours. "Okay, deal. Are you staying, or am I bringing you back?"

Priest held up his hand, smiled, "Wait. There's more. I want J.D. Elliott to handle the sale. He's a retired realtor, a Nam vet, and the son of an old friend, so he will get it done quicker. He knows me and he knows the property better than anybody else." Harp was quick to agree. Anything that would speed up the process was fine with him.

Priest smiled, "In answer to your question, no, you won't be bringing me back. I am going to see my daughter and I will, uh, be staying up there."

"Okay, I just need to let Tommy McArthur know about the whole deal. He will be overseeing the reopening of this place. He's as ready as I am to get away from the Battle."

Priest's face lit up. "You mean Tommy "Two Fist" McArthur? He's going to be your manager? I saw him beat Hugo Belinka in eighty-eight. What great hands he had."

"That's him, and I would hate to take him on even today." Harp smiled at the thought.

Priest was quiet, thinking whether he would share a little more information with Harp and decided against it. He stood with some difficulty and shook hands with Harp. With the decision made, he was eager to get going. "All right, Mr. Harper, let's get this ball rolling."

The ball rolled quickly. In a little under a month, the place was Harp's. Elliott had done a great job pulling it all together. They sat in Priest's kitchen with all the paperwork ready to sign. Harp noticed that Elliott seemed unhappy with the deal. He was regarding Harp with suspicion as the documents were signed. He had already asked Priest if this was what he really wanted to do. Harp could see that what he really wanted to know was why Priest was selling the bar to Harp and why the price was so low. Priest had said nothing about the trip to Rochester, so Harp took the cue and said nothing himself.

When it was done and the last folder full of documents had been signed, Harp pushed the stack of bills totaling $295,000 toward Edgar Priest. They were in packs of hundreds, fifty to the pack. Priest pushed four packs to Elliott, who objected and pushed two back. Priest said, "Goddammit, John, take the money. It's the last time I'll get to pay you for all your help over the years."

Elliott stared intently at Priest, then nodded. "Okay, Ed, but you got to keep me informed on just what the hell you've got planned." He was obviously worried.

Priest lied, "You know I will, buddy." He would not meet Elliott's eyes. Elliott glared at Harp. He knew something was going unsaid here and felt with considerable resentment that Harp knew what it was.

Harp watched the interchange, noting Elliott's suspicion. He couldn't blame him, but he was not about to convey a suspicion he himself had about Priest's motives. Perhaps both knew that Priest had reached a much bigger decision than that represented by the pile of documents on the table.

With Priest's approval, he and Tommy had used the month during the closing process to get the place ready. It was the final step in Priest's separation from his former establishment and this phase of his life. It would now be known as *Vet LZ*, the Veterans Landing Zone. Priest said he kind of liked it. He said with some sadness that he wished he could hang out there.

As for the upstairs residence, Priest told Harp that he had no use for the contents and suggested that Harp either live there, donate it all, or find a renter. Harp offered to pay Priest for the contents and Priest declined, saying there was nothing there worth selling. Priest added that there was a large storage space in the back where he and his brother Hal had been putting stuff for years. He remembered tools for maintaining the building, old advertising, and a lot of hunting equipment from when he and Hal were avid hunters long ago. They just called it their junk room. Out of respect for the former owner's privacy, Harp had not closely inspected the residence portion of the building in any detail. There would be plenty of time for that later.

They left for Rochester at 8 a.m. Tuesday. Priest was wearing a very old suit with a tie that was about seven inches wide. There was a Bronze Star pin in the lapel. They were in Harp's Ford Expedition, all of whose functions he still did not understand, and he still could not operate the radio from the complicated steering wheel. It was important to get there before 5, Priest said, because she would still be at work. He didn't want to see her because the situation was pretty hopeless, he told Harp.

Harp asked why.

Priest didn't answer for a long time. "She thinks I murdered her husband Leland," Priest finally said with a shrug.

Harp, for once, was rendered speechless. He opened and closed his mouth but said nothing.

Priest smiled at Harp's reaction and continued. "I did shoot him, but it was an accident. Leland and I were deer hunting up in central P.A. and the damned idiot refused to wear the day-glow stuff that points out to everyone in the woods that this is not a goddamned animal." Priest sighed. "He was across this shallow ravine, and he was supposed to stay in one spot that we agreed on. We were waiting for deer to come down the ravine. In his damned layered brown gear he was pretty near invisible, but I knew where he was, so it was okay. I wouldn't shoot that way no matter what." Priest shook his head. "Then, for some godforsaken reason, he went to the top of the ravine and started down the middle toward where I was sitting. I saw this deer coming through the trees plain as day, waited, and took my shot." Of course, it was Leland. It was a perfect shot. I blew his head off. Didn't hurt the meat at all." Priest laughed at the irony.

Harp winced at the thought. "Well, hell, Ed, who could blame you for that?"

Priest snapped, "I'll tell you who: my daughter. And, my two grandchildren who listen only to her." He added, "The cops found that I was not in the wrong. They all agreed that Leland was a complete idiot."

Harp offered lamely, "Maybe in time things will work out."

"Not a chance. I never got along with Leland. He was a loser. Couldn't keep a job. Gambled. Messed around. But, she loved him and I made the mistake of expressing my low opinion too often. They thought I hated him so much that I took him hunting just so I could shoot him." Priest laughed bitterly.

Harp was trying to understand Priest's present mission. "So why are we driving to see her today?"

"We are not trying to see her. As a matter of fact, I will probably never see her again," Priest said. Harp heard the catch in his voice as Priest put down the beginning of a sob. "There is one more thing I can do. I can give her the money from the sale, which she can use to pay off her debts and maybe buy some stuff for the kids."

"Okay, then what?" Harp asked.

"Then I am going to visit my wife's grave."

"Then what?"

"Then I want you to mind your own damned business and go back to Trenton and have fun running my old saloon."

Harp shrugged. This was something he was going to do anyway. "Roger."

They rode silently as Harp drove North into New York and through the striking Finger Lakes region. Both minds were too busy to enjoy the verdant hills, lakes, and valleys. They hit the outskirts of Rochester on schedule about six hours after leaving Trenton. Priest steered Harp through streets of old but nicely kept homes directly to a very nice two-story cottage that had a slightly run-down look.

Harp pulled to the curb in front of the house. Without pre-amble, Priest left the truck, carrying the money in an ordinary cloth grocery bag. He confidently walked down a narrow side-walk that ran alongside the house and disappeared around the back. He was gone no more than two minutes when he walked back around the corner and approached the truck. He was car-rying a portrait in a medium sized wooden frame.

He showed the picture to Harp. It was a pleasant looking woman with two younger girls. "This is my daughter and my grandchildren. I think it's a fair trade, don't you? I leave $275,000 and take one picture." Priest laughed and sat staring at the im-ages. Harp waited. Priest then directed, "Okay, let's go to the cemetery. My wife is waiting."

Harp followed directions again. It was cold but looking to be a very nice morning with clear skies. They were soon at the entrance to a very large city cemetery. Priest directed Harp to stop at the gate. Priest got out and opened the rear door and took his small overnight bag. Carrying the bag and the picture, he walked around to the driver's side and waited as Harp rolled down his window. "Can you find your way back to Trenton from here?"

Harp replied, "No problem. You going to be okay?"

Priest turned to study the monuments of this final resting place for thousands. "Actually, this is the most 'okay' I've been in years." He put his hand through the window and Harp shook it. "You came along at just the right time, Mr. Harper, and I deeply appreciate it." He stepped back and smiled, "Have a good trip back, enjoy your new establishment, and," he smiled and pointed his hand like a gun, "keep your powder dry." Priest walked away with a new liveliness, as if he were in a hurry to get somewhere. Harp watched until the old man was out of sight, lost among the tombstones.

Harp thought he understood why he wasn't bringing Priest back. He knew the old pistol was in Priest's small bag. He also knew that it was none of his damned business.

He was back in his condo at 10, wondering again what the hell kind of world it was that would bring an old veteran all by himself to a cold, lonely cemetery.

11

Harp could not know the degree of shock he would soon experience when he awoke early the next morning to a cold, bright day. He got out of bed and showered while thinking of the many things he and Tommy had to do. He laughed to himself. He was a regular tycoon now with two businesses to run! He strode briskly first to the Battle and let himself in. The morning crew had not yet arrived. Harp looked with disgust at the changes that had been made. There was a new, larger LED television in place of that fine old black and white. The sticky, broken pool table was gone. It had been replaced by a long dining table with cute beer lights overhead. There were new napkin holders on the drink rail and even some little umbrellas for fruity drinks on the back bar. The kielbasa, pickled eggs, and pig's feet were gone. He shook his head and went to the office. All this was the work of their new manager, Neal Reynolds.

Tommy and Harp had agreed that they needed to hire someone more "in tune with the times" to operate the Battle in a way suitable for the "in" crowd. Neal was doing a great job. He was a slightly built guy with thick glasses and a limp, but he came highly recommended and was a genius at reading the needs of the clientele. Under his management, they were making lots of money. Didn't matter. Harp still hated what was happening. He couldn't wait to open the Vet LZ. He swore that *this* one would remain quiet, dark, and dull. There would be kielbasa, pickled eggs, and pig's feet. No fucking drink umbrellas. He was wrong again.

One of the first chores on his list was to get something done as a result of now having the apartment over the new bar. He didn't quite know what to do with the rest of it, but there was one part of the apartment that he could use right away. He had just gotten another bill for his storage unit and decided that he would move the few things remaining there into the upstairs junk room. The only things left at the old unit were clothes, helmets, vests, belts, even some civvie wear that he had accumulated over a long military career. He didn't know why he kept most of this stuff. He would never use it again. He couldn't remember for sure, but he thought there was a box with all his medals and citations. He retrieved his SUV from his assigned condo parking spot and drove the couple of miles to the storage center.

Harp, thinking about all he had to do today, was distracted as he removed the lock from the sliding metal door to his unit and pulled it up and out of the way. He was apprehensive about what he would find, knowing that those two spooks had found this hiding place long ago. Harp had no idea what all they had taken or messed with. The first thing he saw took his breath away. Literally. He leaned against the door frame in shock with eyes closed, shaking his head, trying to understand what he was seeing, trying to arrange the thoughts and pictures now flashing like a fast forward slide show in his mind.

There, right where he had left it, was the desert tan, highly irregular, treacherous foot locker that Harp had very illegally spirited out of Pakistan many years ago, and more recently out of the small town of Bardburg, PA, just three years ago. The tools in this container were tools of death, and he had used most of them in both places. Harp slid to a sitting position on the floor leaning against the wall of the storage unit, staring at the thing. He was trying to grasp what its being here meant. He had believed totally that it had been confiscated by the Feds.

His mind was trying to work out all the implications of its presence here. If the locker was still here, that means those bastards either didn't find it — or they found it and left it here. If they didn't find it, they did not have the conclusive evidence tying him to the death of Adam Willarde. If they did not have that evidence, then the plan to force him to assassinate the President was a huge bluff. If he fell for this bluff, then he needlessly ran for months across the country to escape their plot — thinking they could find him any day. He could be killed any day. He could go to prison any day which, for him, was the same as death. (As it came to pass, they *did* find him. And Harp killed them both. He was wounded again in the process. They shot him in the right leg, the one already mangled by shrapnel.)

Harp crawled over to the tan container. He was afraid to open it but knew he had to. The combination was burned into his memory. It still worked. He flipped up the lid. It was all there — the expended 50-caliber cartridge that these professional liars had brought into the Battle those long months ago, the one that supposedly had his fingerprints. Theirs had been a fake. The cartridge he had actually used was right here in front of him. The military Barrett rifle with the damning fingerprints that he had used to eliminate Adam Willarde was right here.

Those bastards had claimed they had it in their possession. They had *nothing* tying him to those actions! And he had believed them! He had believed them enough to desperately escape Trenton under an assumed identity and travel the country for many weeks on the run. Just to be sure, he carefully dug through the contents and studied every surface of the damned thing. There was no RFID tag, sticker, label, etc. Nothing.

Harp jumped to his feet and began loud cursing. "Those bastards! Those miserable sons of bitches! Those lying motherfuckers!" They worked for a clandestine agency that was so hidden they functioned pretty much autonomously. They were under no governmental oversight. They could protect or end lives as they saw fit. (They did the latter quite often all over the world and joked about it.) They knew about Harp's special ability for ultra-long shots because he had been reluctantly drafted by them on a secret mission to take out a terrorist in Pakistan. Harp had hit the target from a distance of about a half mile. It was one of those military things that the public will never know about and even the U.S. Government doesn't want to know about. Harp ended up with the locker when they failed to return from an off-the-books mission while they were still in Pakistan.

Harp had successfully escaped that country on his own and sent the locker home to the States under a fake name. He claimed it from an Army Depot after his discharge. He used the tools in this deadly container locker while defending the lives of his crew and his beautiful lawyer lover when their lives were threatened by Adam Willarde over in Bardburg. Willarde wanted the land Harp had inherited at any cost. It had cost Willarde his life. Harp took it.

The two spooks had convinced Harp that the tan locker had

an RFID tag and had been found from the air. They said Harp had two choices: he could do what they wanted—or he could go to jail. Harp took the third choice. He ran. Now he knows that they did not have a damned thing on him and a gullible Harp had believed them. He was disgusted with himself.

It was while he was running that he found the real intent of these agents. They needed a marksman, a sniper, to assassinate the President. It was in the papers. He was in Arizona traveling in a camper as Kenneth Nelson, a recently widowed man on a road trip of remembrance. The two rogue agents had failed to mention that the plan was for the sniper to be discovered and killed *before* he could fire on the President. It was a setup. A rogue operation. That sniper was supposed to be Harp. Obviously, they had found someone else to do it. And, as planned, that person had been slain by the Secret Service and a thankful President was thus convinced to allot more money to that agency. The plan worked. It cost only one life. That was supposed to be me, he thought, bitterly. Harp wondered who the poor sucker was who had been similarly trapped into this deadly mission.

He decided to leave the locker where it was for now. He didn't want the damned thing in the junk room over the Vet LZ. All he knew was that he had to get rid of it. He should have done it years ago. He pulled the door down noisily, slamming it against the floor of the storage building and fastening the lock in place. He was totally disgusted with himself for being so gullible. He kicked the door.

12

That evening, after working with Tommy on the finishing touches to his new establishment, he left for his usual walk home. It was 8 p.m. on a cold, dark night with splashes of color under each street light. He was tired and distracted from the events of the day. He wasn't as alert as he should have been. He had been carrying an old 32 automatic since Dominic's confrontation. It had been given to Tommy by Manny Obregata's wife, and Harp had been carrying it since the warning about Arturo Donetti's almost certain revenge. It was right there in his pants pocket. His hands were in his coat pockets. It didn't matter anyway.

Harp was alert enough to note with caution a person stepping from a doorway several yards away. It was a well-dressed handsome man carrying a suitcase. The man was talking to someone inside the door. He laughed and loudly said he would call as soon as he got there. He shouted his goodbye over his shoulder and smiled easily and nodded at Harp as he passed. Harp nodded and kept walking. As soon as Harp had walked past, the man whirled and, in one quick motion, put a revolver inches from the back of Harp's head and very quickly pulled the trigger twice. Harp had a moment when he knew something was wrong, there was a loud noise, and then there was nothing.

The shooter was satisfied that his aim had been good. There was a burst of blood, scalp, and hair from the back of Harp's head and a burst of blood from the front. Obviously a through and through. Harp fell limply and landed on his face on the sidewalk. With gloved hand, the shooter threw the untraceable pistol next to the body and calmly walked to a nearby sedan and drove off. There had been no one in the doorway, and there was nothing in the suitcase. It was the perfect ruse. He knew Harp's walking route, and he had been waiting for the right time. Arty would be pleased.

Several calls went in to 911. There were now bystanders standing around Harp's body. None dared to touch him. From the amount of blood and the gaping head wounds front and back, it was obvious to all of them that this guy was stone cold dead.

13

From a lifetime in war with many injuries, some critical, Harp knew where he was when he regained a cloudy level of consciousness. He could hear the beeps, sense the connections, and smell the smells. His throat hurt, so he knew he had been intubated. He had been in places like this many times before. He knew he was in a hospital and he knew he was in intensive care. He knew he couldn't see and that his hands were tied down. What he didn't know was *why* he was there. After puzzling over this very briefly, he went back to sleep. He was dreaming of explosions, blood, bodies torn apart, trucks burning, aiming a weapon, then running, running, running. Somewhere in there was his own pain, but it was everywhere. It was so large that he was swimming in it. The blackness that came again was welcome.

Also from a lifetime at war, Harp was a walking, talking display of the many different kinds of metal that the human body could accommodate. He carried an uncounted number of pieces in arms, legs, torso, and head. Some were put there by doctors, and some were put there by the enemy. One of those pieces of metal was a titanium plate on the occipital bone on the right side in the back of Harp's scull near the lambdoid suture. It replaced a quarter-sized piece of bone, which had been shattered by shrapnel and medically removed as too splintered to ever properly heal.

Because Harp had been wearing his old peacoat, the thick seam at the edge of the heavy woolen collar brought about a very minor deflection of the first bullet, bending it slightly upward to where it hit that titanium plate, which further deflected it up and out, leaving a large vertically-oriented jagged hole in Harp's scalp. The force of the strike on the titanium plate twisted his head just enough so that the second shot penetrated his scalp over his ear and traveled between the scalp and skull to a point about two inches above Harp's right eye where it exited, again with a burst of blood and tissue. When Harp limply fell on his face, he fractured his left cheekbone on the cold concrete surface of the sidewalk.

When Harp awoke again, it was to the sound of men talking. A familiar voice asked, "What do you think doctor, will he come out of it?"

"We don't know. I've told you this before. He is a lucky man. He was shot in the head twice, but his injuries were survivable and treatable." Harp was aware of the doctor touching, moving, adjusting all the tubes and wires around and in his body. His eyes were covered with something, so he couldn't see anything but a faint white light. The oxygen line taped under his nose was adjusted. He felt the covers being moved below his waist. He felt other tugs of things connected to his head. He wanted to say something when he felt the doctor's hands on his penis making sure the catheter was still in place and draining properly, but he couldn't speak because of this horrible tube down his throat.

Then the voice he knew again, pleading. "Doc, it's been days. He's a tough guy. What's wrong?"

The doctor patiently explained, "You must understand that these are severe injuries. The physical trauma was significant. Even with no penetration of the occipital, there was an unknown amount of blunt force trauma to that part of the brain. We never know in cases like this whether there is fixable damage or permanent damage. And, we won't know until we begin to communicate with an alert person." The doctor turned to leave.

Harp was listening. He now knew what had happened. He had been shot in the head twice. It seemed like just knowing this awakened the pain that had been there on the edge of his consciousness but not yet realized. Now, for the first time, he became aware of an agony that seemed to envelop his head. It would move from the back to the front to his cheek to his eyes. It was too much. He wanted to sleep, but he didn't want to dream. He went back to sleep. He dreamed again of war.

"Do we know how long they'll keep a guard at the door?" Bonny asked. Army veteran Sergeant Marion Bondurant had that voice Harp had vaguely recognized before. Bonny had left the farm he and Phil Weeks had bought in North Carolina to stand guard over his brother warrior Senior Master Sergeant Horace B. "Harp" Harper, who now lay unconscious in this hospital bed. Bonny was determined that he would stand watch each night until his friend was somehow safe and well. A daytime attempt in a very busy hospital was extremely unlikely. That's when he slept.

"I have no idea. You will have to talk to Detective Carroll about that." The doctor left. Carroll had warned the hospital and the friends visiting Harp that Arturo Donetti now knew that Harp was still alive. The failed attempt on Harp's life had again been the subject of lurid stories in the various media. Arty Boots wouldn't forget and wouldn't let it go. He would try again. For this attempt, Arty was comfortably ensconced in his villa on the coast of Italy at the time it occurred. Again, he expressed shock and dismay at the lack of safety in his wonderful hometown. He blamed it on the liberal policies of the mayor and chief of police. He said somebody should do something.

When Harp next awoke, another day had passed and he had a clearer mind. He made a sound. The tube was gone, but he was still getting oxygen. He didn't know what time it was, but he could see no light through the gauze bandages. He heard the squeak of a vinyl cushion and suddenly someone was right there leaning over him. "Sarge, goddamn, Sarge, are you okay?" His voice was high and tense.

Harp felt a tremendous sense of relief and gratitude as he realized it was Bonny. He was glad that this loyal soldier could not see the tears in his eyes. With a hoarse croak he answered. "Jesus, Bonny, relax. I'm alive, I think."

Bonny was practically dancing in relief and grinning ear to ear. "We didn't know. All this time we didn't know if you were going to pull out of this. I shoulda known that you were too damned stubborn to let a couple of shots to the head kill you." He had taken Harp's hand in both of his giant mitts and stood there holding it. "Everybody's been here. Weeks came up. Even Kowalski came by. She cried when she saw you. She called you a fucking idiot and said she hoped you died. Then she cried some more. I think she loves you." Harp slowly shook his head in disbelief. Bonny went on. "This guy Tommy was here. He said don't worry about the business. He and that lawyer Weaver will take care of everything."

Harp sensed the smile in Bonny's voice. He smiled too—as much as he could—but he knew they had more important things to discuss. "Bonny, there's no way I can ever pay you back for this. It is beyond your scope of duty. I might have to put you on report." Bonny grinned. Harp's brain was back. "But now I need a detailed sit-rep (Situation Report). Take your time and if you see me fading before you're done, give me a poke. I need to know everything."

Bonny pulled a chair over to the edge of the bed and began quietly talking. His experience reporting complete details for mission planning kicked in. "Five days ago, at about 2025 hours, an unknown person put two 32 caliber slugs into the back of your head as you were walking home on Cobb Street. It is suspected that this person was in the employ of one Arturo Donetti. That comes from a Detective Jay Carroll who has been here to see you several times. You were brought to this hospital in critical condition and went immediately into emergency surgery. One slug was slightly deflected by the collar of your coat and further deflected by the titanium plate in the back of your head, which none of us knew about." Harp shrugged. Bonny continued. "It is thought that this movement caused the second bullet to enter your thick head at an angle and tunnel between your skull and scalp and exit one and three-quarter inches over your right eye. You fell unconscious to the sidewalk, landing on your stomach with the left side of your face hitting the concrete with enough force to fracture your left cheek and orbital bones. Both fractures are partial and won't need surgical repair."

Bonny paused. Harp was suddenly consumed with thirst.

71

His mouth was dry and throat sore. Harp asked, "Will they let you give me some water?"

"Yeah, they said it's okay now. They took the breathing tube out yesterday." Bonny held a covered cup and straw while Harp greedily sucked cold water." The motion hurt his left cheek but he didn't care.

"God, that tastes good." It felt wonderful on his sore throat. Harp then grimly directed, "Keep going."

"The surgical staff here spent a few hours sewing everything back together. I don't know how many stiches you have holding your scalp together. You had the explosive in/out wound on the back of your head and they had to open up the path of the bullet from back to front to stop any inside bleeding. You lost a shitload of blood, by the way, so you're going to be pretty weak for a while. The exit wound on your right forehead was large, but they were able to pull the edges back together. Because of your incredibly thick skull, neither projectile actually penetrated into your brain. You will have a shitload of scars, including a large hairless vertically-oriented patch on the back of your head that reaches all along the path of the bullet on the side of your head and around the exit wound. Right now, your whole head is shaved and on the left side you have no eyebrow. You will have some serious scars."

"Fuck a bunch of scars. Who cares," Harp commented, expecting the worst was yet to come.

Bonny continued. "The effect of all these wounds is that your already ugly head is covered with bandages with a lot of drains. The bandages in the back have a little spacer built in so the wounds won't touch anything when you are lying on your back. The ones on your cheek are designed to keep the bones in place while they knit. Your eyes are covered for now because of the way the bandages are placed. You are hooked up for pulse, blood pressure, oxygen, saline drip, and intravenous feeding. They have removed some of the thicker bandages and drains already because the bullet wounds appear to be healing nicely. They expect that, once everything is healed, there should be no effect on your vision."

Harp was getting tired and sighed in relief. That's what he had been most worried about. Bonny went on, "In related issues, the VA has been notified and has already agreed to cover the costs of all this. As to when you will be released, I don't have any idea. Which brings up another problem. They have pulled your police protection, and we are now on our own." Harp noticed and deeply appreciated the "our." "When you're up to it, we are going to get you out of here and someplace safe while you recover."

What Bonny didn't say was that the doctor had said emphatically that Harp could not be moved. The occipital lobe in Harp's brain had been seriously bruised, so a drain was necessary. He explained that this was the part of the brain that controlled the ability to read and recognize printed words along with other aspects of vision. To move him too quickly could jeopardize the healing process. Bonny had made a command decision, however. He concluded that the first priority was to get Harp to a safe place.

Being dead would also compromise Harp's ability to read.

"Who is 'we'?" Harp asked.

Bonny said while smiling, "Good old Kip has got a place. It seems his father wanted to get him started in the business, so he gave him a few properties."

"Gave him properties?" Harp asked. He was getting tired.

"It seems that young Kip wasn't kidding when he said he was going to be loaded. He and his father are now getting along, so the old man moved up his inheritance. Kip now owns a few apartment buildings. He has a very confidential pad in one of these places. I don't know where and I don't want to. I need to preserve my deniability. We talked about your situation, and he agreed we should take you there as soon as you can be moved. Donetti is going to try again, and we just can't watch you around the clock here." Bonny looked slightly uncomfortable. "And, I hate to even bring it up, but me and Weeks got way too much to do on the farm. He needs me back there."

Harp suddenly felt incredibly selfish. Maybe he could have avoided all this. Now, his squad, his brothers, were having to make huge sacrifices to take care of him. "Ah, hell, Bonny, go on and go back down there. I'm gonna be fine. I'll be out of here in no time. I can recuperate anywhere. I promise I will sit there with my sidearm and nail any Donetti asshole who comes through the door."

Bonny smiled. It was exactly what he expected Harp to say. "No way, Sarge. I won't leave until you are moved and safe." Harp teared up again. Again he was glad his eyes didn't show.

"There's more on the sit-rep." Bonny said. He was grinning. "You are wearing pretty blue diapers and you have a catheter inserted. They changed these things while I was in the room."

Harp said, "Oh, shit, I'm sorry, man. I know it's embarrassing to see that shit."

Bonny was really grinning now. "No, that wasn't what was embarrassing. I was embarrassed to see how tiny your dick is."

It took Harp a few seconds to get it. Bonny was waiting

and, when he saw the barb sink home, broke out laughing. Harp starting laughing and wincing and said, "You realize, of course, that when I get out of here I am going to have to kick your ass."

14

He fell asleep smiling. Bonny was smiling also as he settled in to catch a few winks. But, those years of half-asleep/half-awake brought him to his feet when he heard a slight noise in the hall outside the door. There hadn't been that many visits in the middle of the night. It was 2:30 a.m. As Bonny was moving toward the door, he saw an arm come first through the door, and the arm was carrying an automatic with silencer attached. It was aimed at Harp. Bonny chopped the arm just as a shot was fired. Then, the extended barrel and Bonny's raw strength made it easy for him to twist the weapon in and out of the shooter's grip with his thumb between the trigger and firing pin. Bonny's experience in man-to-man combat also made it a simple thing to pull the shooter into the room, dislocate his shoulder by tucking his arm behind his neck and then break it. All of which took about five seconds. He was then easily rendered unconscious by an expert vegus nerve strike.

All was done in silence because of the shooter's determination to make no noise. The pistol had a quality silencer making only a mild snap — like a hand slapping a leg. Bonny dropped the shocked assassin to the floor and rushed over to check on Harp.

He saw the hole in the mattress under Harp's head and sighed in relief. Harp was still sleeping soundly. Bonny hated to wake him up, but the time had come for a strategic retreat—double time. The presence of a replacement body would help Bonny's plan.

It took only about half an hour and a lot of patience by both men. Harp was soon wearing the shooter's clothes, including the doctor's coat along with the fake badge. He even had a stethoscope hanging around his neck. The dressing over his left eye was pushed up enough so he could see. Though he could barely walk, he knew the importance of getting to someplace safe. He was weakly collapsed in the chair trying to gather strength for what lay ahead. The assassin was in the hospital bed covered in sheets with his hands strapped down, his feet tied with medical tape, his head wrapped in bandages, including a gag taped over his mouth. With the sheets pulled up to his nose, it could easily be Harp still lying there. Bonny had even put the small pulse monitor on the end of one of the shooter's fingers. Bonny wiped his prints then wrapped the shooter's fingers around the pistol, leaving only his prints on the gun. He then put it under the pillow.

When all was arranged, Bonny did one more thing and then helped Harp from the chair. Harp grinned when he saw what Bonny had done. "Bonny, I think this is the guy who got me. He was coming out of a door talking and laughing so I thought he was nothing. He fooled me." Harp started to shake his head and quickly realized he wouldn't be doing that for a while.

Bonny saw his weakness and held him up. "Can you see okay?" He was really worried about the next step.

Harp nodded, "Yeah, but if I move my head too fast, it spins."

Bonny nodded in understanding but said, "You have got to

hold it together, Sarge. You've been walking wounded as bad as this before, so I know you can do it.'

"I'll hold up my end." Harp said. Bonny knew he would.

The experienced battle-tested sergeant had worked on this plan from the moment Harp had entered the hospital. It was all part of military training on scenario response. You imagine possible scenarios then figure ways to respond. One had Harp wandering down the hall pushing an intravenous stand. This was better. "Okay, here's the plan. I'm going to go out the door to the right down the hall to the nurse's station and chat with the night nurse. I've done it before. I will try to block her vision of this door. You are going to walk out of the room and go to the left. Walk like you have been here a hundred times. Turn up your collar and carry the patient chart." Bonny's voice changed. It was now the mission voice. "This is the hard part. There will be an exit sign on your right. You must take the exit, not the elevator, and go down three flights of stairs to the garage. Take your time. Spend energy slowly." Harp took a deep breath and made the thumbs up sign. It hurt too much to nod. "When I see you walk out of the room, I am going to leave the nurse's station and take the elevator to the garage. I will get my car and probably be at the door to the stairs by the time you get there. You get in the back seat and crash."

Bonny went to the door and paused. "It's 0300 hours. We shouldn't run into anybody." It was only Harp's promise to Bonny that kept him moving in the stairwell—that plus the fact that the feeling of weakness just plain pissed him off. He heard a door open and close below him, but no one came up the stairs. He had to stop at the first-floor landing and hold tight to the railing for a few long seconds before going the last steps down to the garage door. By the time he got to the garage, he was barely able to stand. He opened the door to the garage just as Bonny stopped. Harp managed to get the rear door of the car open. He dropped heavily into the seat, closed the door, and fell sideways. With a symphony of chirping, squealing, roaring echoing in the garage, Bonny's car exited and headed north. Harp was out.

When Harp awoke again, it was to the sound of Bonny and Kip talking. The cars were side by side in a highway rest area. It was still dark. Harp could tell their conversation was relaxed, so he didn't have to worry. He was too tired to move. He slept and waited. Then his shoulder was being gently shaken. "Sarge, wake up." Harp stirred slightly. His shoulder was shaken less gently. "Come on Sarge, we got to move."

Memories of other missions when he was dead tired finally drove Harp to drag himself up from his deep slumber. He pushed himself erect. He was still in Bonny's car. He mumbled, "Okay, I'm with you. Hey, Kip. Good to see you."

Kip leaned into the car and took Harp's hand to help him stand. He was shocked to see his most admired sergeant in this condition. "You too, Sarge." They did an awkward man hug. "Come on, get in the back and lie down. We'll talk later."

After he had followed those directions, Bonny stood at the rear of the car under the open hatch and said his goodbyes. "Sarge, I'm going back to the farm. I should be there mid-day. The police will come to talk to me. Fuck 'em. I will tell them what happened in the hospital, why we left, and how we left. I will tell them I helped you leave the hospital and I dropped you off on your orders at this rest stop and don't know where you are." Harp understood. Bonny continued, "From this point, only two people will know where you are. That's you and Kip.

Even I won't know. From all his experience, Kip is pretty sure he can keep your wounds clean and dressed. He will be your nurse. He can call me and Weeks if something goes seriously south." He stopped and smiled. "It's been a trip, Sergeant Harper." He saluted and stuck out his hand.

Harp took his hand in both of his and said, "Words don't cover it, Bonny." Bonny waved and left for North Carolina.

Kip closed the hatch and drove away from the rest area. Talking to the rear-view mirror, he said, "We got about a half hour, so sack out, Sarge. I'll get you out of your bunk when we get there." Harp slept.

15

The doctor was furious. The hospital director was furious. Arty Boots was furious. Detective Carroll was curious. The nurse was scared stiff. That night nurse, who was on duty when Harp disappeared, had gone on her 5 a.m. rounds looking forward to getting home and fixing breakfast for the kids before they left for school. She found a stranger in a bed that had been recently occupied by a patient still in serious but stable condition. The person in the bed was unconscious and wearing just his shorts. His hands had been strapped down and his feet tied. When she moved the sheet that had covered his lower face, she found that he was also gagged with wide strips of bandage tape. Written on his forehead were the words: *under pillow.* Then, on left and right cheeks: *Call* and *911.* Still in shock, she looked under the pillow and saw with horror the large pistol with its long silencer attached. She jumped away from the bed and did as directed. She rushed back to her station and called 911 and the night supervisor. She was a professional. She updated her charts while waiting for the shit to come down. It was simple: *5:06 a.m. Patient H.B. Harper, Room 2257, not present. Unknown unconscious male occupying bed. Firearm under his pillow. Supervisor notified. Police notified.*

At 6 a.m. in the West Wing Ward Four, they were standing in line to question the nurse. Carroll walked down the hall to find this small group of staffers busy trying to find the right place to assign the blame. Their concern was not necessarily the well-being of the patient but the insurance ramifications of having a patient missing before the bills were paid. The hospital had been searched, and he was truly gone. The lawyers had not shown up yet but were on their way. Carroll went straight to Harp's room. He found what the nurse had found. He read the message on the shooter's head and chuckled. He carefully checked under the pillow and whistled. He knew whose fingerprints they would find. He found the bullet hole in the side of the mattress and mouthed a silent *wow*. The difference was that Carroll knew immediately what had happened. He shook his head and smiled in admiration for Bonny. But now, it was a crime scene. Attempted murder by the guy in the bed. The bullet would be in the mattress and no doubt match the pistol. With this guy's prints on the gun and the bullet in the mattress, it would be an easy charge to back up.

Carroll touched nothing else and called it in. He studied the room as he waited for the tech crew to show up. He took a picture of the guy in the bed and sent it in for ID. It came back quickly. This was a professional. He was a suspect in several hits but nothing ever stuck. His name was Harvey "Frat Boy" Tanner. The word was that he was from a good family and a college graduate. He was first coerced into a life of crime over gambling debts but found that he liked it. His handsome, preppy appearance fooled many victims into thinking that he was harmless. He proved them wrong. It was thought that he was mostly freelance but could very likely have been hired by Arty Boots for this hit. And Carroll did not doubt for a minute that this was a hit job. He knew that Arty wasn't going to quit.

Tanner woke up while several people dressed in all white plastic suits were busy lifting, poking, dusting everything in the room. His hands were bagged. "What the hell! What the hell are you doing?" he said loudly. Then he tried to lift his arms and became aware that his arm was broken and dislocated and screamed. Everyone, including Carroll, was startled by the scream. It was a genuine scream of pain. They called for a doctor who, after a brief examination, described Tanner's injuries. Carroll again thought of Bonny with admiration. Goddam, he thought, he took the gun away from a professional and, in the process, trashed the guy's arm.

They unstrapped Tanner's arms and removed the tape from his feet. The doctor said that Tanner's arm had to be treated. He could not be taken from the hospital until after that had been done. They would reset his shoulder and put a cast on his arm, then he could be taken away. He was taken for treatment under heavy guard, complaining all the way about his innocence and threatening to sue the hospital and the police. He still hadn't seen his face but was wondering why everyone looked at him and grinned. His blood froze when he saw his visage in a hand-held mirror. He knew he would now be a laughing stock among the cruel people he served.

With Tanner gone, and while the crime scene guys did their work, the detective finally got to talk to the nurse. She described the events of the morning again. She said she was busy at her desk around 3 a.m. when Mr. Bondurant came down the hall to chat with her on his way out. He only stood there for a minute or so, then said he was going home. He went to the elevator and waved at her as he stepped in. She saw him leave. She went back to work on her charts. At 5:06 on her 5 a.m. rounds, she entered Harper's room and found the strange male unconscious in Harper's bed. Harper was gone. She saw what was written on Tanner's face and then notified her supervisor and called 911. She added that she couldn't imagine how Mr. Harper could have gotten himself out of bed and out of the hospital.

Carroll summarized what he had. He had a known professional hit man. He had proof of another attempt on the life of Harper. He had the weapon with the shooter's prints on it. He had the bullet from the mattress. He could put Tanner away just on that evidence. What he didn't have was the intended victim. Carroll suspected that Harper was by now safely away. He hoped he would stay that way. They didn't stand a chance of pinning this on Arturo Donetti. As for Harper, he hadn't committed any crime that Carroll could see other than skipping on a hospital bill. Even that, they say, was a non-issue because it would be covered by the Veteran's Administration.

It was now 11:07 a.m. Carroll was tired. He was going to grab some shuteye in his office then call one Marion "Bonny" Bondurant. He looked forward to that interview with pleasure.

16

The next time Harp woke up was at the same time Arty Boots awoke. But it was 6 a.m. in Philly—and noon in Rome. The difference was, Harp was hiding in a modern flat in Philadelphia and Arty was hiding in a villa in Italy. Each had a similar idea, however. Arty was desperate to kill Harp so he could come home and take care of business. Harp knew he had to kill Arty before Arty killed him. Arty had to be out of the country to have a rock-solid alibi. Harp had to stay hidden to stay alive.

Harp was awake and felt human again for the first time since he had been shot. The pain was there but it was now no worse than what he had been living with from other injuries over the years. He didn't try to get up. He took his time feeling the bandages and, as men will do in some atavistic way of measuring readiness, pressing too hard on his wounds just to see how much they hurt. He found that his cheek didn't hurt much at all. The back and side of his head were tender but didn't hurt unless he pushed extra hard. Oddly enough, the one that was still really sensitive was the exit wound over his eye. He winced inwardly at the thought of how it would look when it was uncovered. He would have to be patient with that one.

He continued the self-examination by moving his arms and legs and twisting his torso. Everything seemed to work. He decided to get up. He wanted to get to the bathroom and get rid of the damned diaper. The first try to stand didn't work. He fell back on the edge of the bed with his head spinning. After waiting a couple of minutes, he stood again but this time slowly. It worked. He took one step, then another, and found he was gaining confidence with each step. He made it to the bathroom. He badly wanted a shower but then saw his reflection in the mirror. It was clear that he would not be showering any time soon. There were too many stitches. Too much red flesh. He would need a whole head shower cap.

He was looking at a tired old man—a shaggy, unshaven, slumped shouldered, thin wreck of a man with a shaved head covered in white bandages, two black eyes, and slightly yellow teeth. In order of occurrence, Harp was shocked, then dismayed, then discouraged, then determined to recover, and then thoroughly, totally, deeply, pissed at the man who had done this to him. He found a new toothbrush and brushed his teeth for a good five minutes. It hurt his cheek, but he didn't care. It felt wonderful to kill the nest of roaches that had been living in his mouth.

This new anger was like a miracle medicine. He left the bathroom with a determination to be whole again. He began by carefully scouting his surroundings. He found he was in a luxurious flat with three bedrooms, three baths, a small exercise room, a small office, a large open area with a kitchen, TV viewing area, and bar. He was alone. There were floor-to-ceiling windows along the living area wall that looked out upon an ordinary cityscape of medium tall buildings. He had no idea where he was, but those windows made Harp nervous. As a professional, having often been exposed to incoming fire, this openness was not a smart tactic. He was relieved to find a wall switch with curtain open/close positions for both transparent and opaque curtains. He closed the transparent curtains all the way. He would not be visible through those windows during the day. He understood that only Kip knew where he was, and he wanted to keep it that way. He wondered where Kip was.

Harp found plenty of food in the fridge. Kip had been extremely thoughtful in his choices. There were many soft foods that didn't require heavy chewing. Harp was suddenly ravenous. He ate a little of everything and drank some milk. He knew from past experience to go slowly. It still hurt to chew, but not much. He carried a small cup of yogurt and a spoon to a marvelous leather chair and propped up his feet. Harp found the remote and turned on the news. Nothing had changed. The country was still fucked. He sat eating and thinking.

It was thus that a plan began taking shape. He first thought that his goal would be to kill Arturo Donetti. That was quickly changed to *ruin* Arty and *then* kill him. To do this he needed help getting into Arty's world. He was determined that none of his Bardberg squad would be involved in his actions, so he wouldn't ask them for anything. Then a name and a story came to him. He thought it would be worth a try to contact this person just to find out if the desire for revenge against the Donettis was as great as his.

Harp next considered the circumstances of his situation relative to his goals, adding and subtracting factors as they now existed. Only Kip knew where he was. Harp laughed aloud at this thought. Even Harp didn't know where he was. He could think of himself as a man who disappeared. How could that be used? Then, what would be the best way to ruin a wealthy, remorseless, experienced mobster who was no doubt heavily guarded at all times? Then, where could he get the tools necessary to carry out the plan?

Before he could do anything, Harp realized he needed to get back in shape. He knew this was going to take time and misery. He was still relaxing in the wonderful chair when Kip returned. Harp got to his feet as fast as he could and watched Kip enter the kitchen with his arms full of shopping bags. He put the bags on the counter and turned to Harp with a huge smile of pleasure at seeing the old Sarge finally up and about. Harp looked at Kip in wonder. He had first met Wellington Kipling Finch-Smithers IV when Bonny had brought him to that damned farm three years ago. Aged just nineteen, he had been wounded in Afghanistan, losing his left eye and a good part of his cheek. The wound had still been ugly and angry and reached from his forehead all the way to his jawline. That soldier Harp met was also angry and resentful. Through actions taken together to survive, Kip and the others had developed a strong bond with their Sergeant Harper and each felt they owed a great deal to this old soldier. That experience had brought all of them back to a level of mental normalcy, allowing them to walk away from the anger and regret of war and function in a civilian world. Kip quickly strode over and enveloped Harper in a huge but careful hug, which Harp returned.

They stepped back and studied one another, both grinning. "Goddamn, Kip, I wouldn't have known you," Harp said. "Let me look at you." In an affectionate display of familiarity, Harp took Kip's chin in his hand and turned his head to the left and right while studying Kip's face. Kip allowed the study with a grin and let him move his head so that it could be studied from all angles.

"This is amazing! I knew they had gotten to where they could fix just about anything, but this is incredible." Harp was looking at an extremely handsome young man with blond hair and perfect profile whose scars could be seen only if you knew to look for them. Now, instead of a mass of curled flesh where the eye had been, there was an eyebrow, even some eyelashes, and an artificial eye perfectly matching the right eye. Kip, grinning still, patiently waited for Harp to finish examination. "I hate to say it, but you are now almost presentable."

Kip laughed and studied Harp's face in return. "You, on the other hand, with all due respect, look like shit, Sarge."

Harp winced and smiled. "Yeah, I know. I just saw myself in a mirror."

"Well, at least you're going to live. For a while there, we had some doubts."

They stood, just looking at each other comfortably for a moment then Harp said, "I need to sit down. Let's sit and talk." He shuffled to a stool at the kitchen counter while Kip watched with dismay at this sign of weakness and indefensibility in this former warrior.

"Okay, shoot." Kip started putting groceries away.

"Where am I?" Kip laughed at Harp's first question.

"You are in my private suite on the top floor of a ten-story, family-owned building at 5672 S. Ruckett Street in Philadelphia, PA."

"Who knows I'm here?"

"Me. Only me. Not even Bonny. I brought you in on my

private elevator from the garage and no one saw us enter. There are two suites on this floor and the other one is empty. The elevator is coded so only I can use it. You are as safe and secure as we can make you. I haven't told a soul you are here."

"We?" Harp asked.

"When he is questioned about your disappearance, which I'm sure he has been by now, he will honestly say he has no idea where you are. He will say he let you out at a rest stop and has neither seen nor heard from you, all of which is true."

"What about the people back in Trenton who will be asking about me?"

"Bonny told your lawyer Aaron Weaver that everyone and anyone who is asked about your whereabouts to only say, 'I don't know where he is, I haven't heard from him, and I don't know if he is dead or alive.'" Kip added, "Again, all of which is true. They don't know."

Harp said, "Weaver is a good man. I will have to assume that he is taking care of business while I'm gone. At least, I hope so."

Harp was tired again. "Kip, I've about had it for now. I need to hit the sack."

"Best thing for you, Sarge." He came around the counter. "Let me take a look at your head first." As Harp sat on the stool, eyes closed, Kip carefully examined all the bandages for the correct pressure and signs of leakage. Satisfied, he said, "Go ahead and sleep as long as you want. We'll change the bandages when you wake up."

Neither realized that Harp, now in a safe place with almost no pain, would fall into a deep sleep that would last straight through the night and into the following morning.

17

Harp slowly rolled from the luxurious bed and cautiously stood up. He felt fine. He knew he was still weak but now felt ready to begin some serious recuperation. He again wandered through the large suite, now marveling at its richness. He looked at himself in a mirror and was pleased to see that his eyes were now just a little less black, and the swelling around his forehead had lessened. Once again, he pushed on all the damaged spots to find that all were less responsive to the pressure. Goddamn, he thought with pleasure, I think I might actually survive. He walked, hopped a couple of times, did deep knee bends, and waved his arms in circles. None of it hurt, but he collapsed into a chair from the effort.

He felt an incredibly strong need for a shower, but he still had all kinds of bandages around his head. Thinking of how he might do it took him to the kitchen where he found a box of typical kitchen trash bags. Harp pulled a white 13-gallon trash bag over his head and used the ties to enclose it to the point where only one eye, his nose, and his mouth were exposed. He then got into the large glass-enclosed shower with four shower heads running hot water at full pressure and took the longest, most pleasurable shower of his life. He came out of the shower actually singing. He stepped into his bedroom with a towel wrapped around his waist to find Kip standing there with a worried expression on his face. When Harp came through the door, Kip's mouth fell open—first in shock and then in laughing wonder at this strange figure with a wet garbage bag hanging from his head and towel around his waist and nothing else. Kip then started laughing so hard he fell on the bed holding his stomach. Harp was not as amused until he went back and looked in the mirror. Then they were both laughing. It still hurt but not as much.

While Harp dressed, Kip fixed coffee. They sat at the counter contentedly sipping coffee and eating pastries Kip had brought in.

Kip started. "Okay, Sarge, you're looking like you are on the comeback trail. What's next?"

Harp chose his words carefully because he wasn't sure yet how involved he wanted Kip to be in his plans. "Kip, you know that Donetti is not going to quit. He won't be happy until I'm dead. And there ain't a damn thing the law or anybody else can do about it."

Kip nodded agreement with a grimace. "And you can't live any kind of life knowing that he could get to you anytime, anywhere."

"Right." Harp chose his words carefully, "The only chance I have for living *period* is if something happens to Arturo Donetti. It might be another five years, but he will get me if I let him." Harp sat looking intently at Kip following this statement.

Having seen Harp in action and guessing what was coming next, Kip was aware of a decision he would have to make. How far would he go in support of Harp? "Go ahead, Sarge, lay it on me," he said with a grim smile.

"It's simple, Kip. I've got to get him before he gets me." Harp watched Kip's eyes. "You know what I'm talking about here. I have got to find a way."

Kip winced, but he wasn't surprised. "Go on."

Harp elaborated. "I might have been happy one time just to take him out and let that be it. But when I think about this last attempt in the hospital and how close I came to cashing in, I decided that's not enough for this prick. I want to hurt him first and then kill him."

Kip understood. Any kind of assistance or foreknowledge made him an accessory, perhaps even to multiple homicides. Even having Harp in his building would be actionable. He would do anything for Harp and though the squad had already gotten away with the death by explosives of one bad guy, he wasn't sure he wanted to push his luck.

Harp knew his men. He recognized the reluctance in Kip and moved quickly to ease his concern. "Jesus, Kip, you don't have to be part of all that, so quit worrying. It's going to take a long time before I'm ready for action. If it's okay with you, I just want to hide out here until I get back into shape."

The relief on Kip's face was obvious. With tremendous physical and mental effort, he had brought his life around after the life altering wounds he had suffered in Afghanistan. He was finally secure and happy. He would hate to give this hard-won life up now. "Sarge, you can stay here as long as you want. You can have anything you want. Just ask. I am proud to help you." They shook hands to seal the understanding.

"There is one thing, Kip." Harp was finding it hard to explain this next request. "There is a person, a woman, who could help me if she wants to. I want to have her stay here with me for a while, just for a kind of briefing."

Kip looked at Harp with raised eyebrows. Harp responded, "No, asshole, it's not like that. All I can tell you is that she was also very badly hurt by the Donettis. She might have some information I can use in my plan."

Kip shrugged, "It doesn't matter to me who you bring in. It will mean that three people know where you are. You okay with that?"

"I know, and I'm kind of taking a chance, but I just feel like she will welcome the chance to help anybody who will do anything to get back at that bunch," Harp explained.

"I got to trust you know what you're doing, Sarge. It's your call," Kip looked at his watch. "Now I've got some work to do, believe it or not, so I will check with you tonight." He stopped at the door and looked back at Harp in concern.

Harp waved him away. "Go on! I'm good. I'm going back to bed." That's what he did, but it was more of a collapse in bed. Harp fell into a deep dreamless sleep while thinking of Luna Norse.

18

Another month had passed during which Harp had driven himself to a point where he could finally move all parts of his body
normally. He was almost back to normal weight but had a long
way to go to reach his former condition. He had just about worn
out the machines in Kip's small exercise room. He still had mild
headaches periodically and sometimes a strange sense of being
high. The bandages had gotten smaller, but the wound on his
forehead was still troublesome. His hair had grown out to max
military length, but the wounds were very evident.

It was time to make the call.

"Yes, of course I remember you, Mr. Harper," Luna Norse
responded to his question.

"Do you have a minute?" Harp asked. "There's a couple of
things I would like to ask you."

She laughed, "Mr. Harper, right now I have more minutes
than ever." There was a note of bitterness in her voice.

Sensitive to that note, Harp said, "Ah, maybe this is not the
best time, then."

"No, no, I'm sorry. Things have seemed to pile in lately and I
am a little overwhelmed."

Hell, Harp thought. Maybe this isn't a good idea. "Is there anything I can do to help?" he asked, just to say something.

Norse laughed, "If you can get my house sold, get my job back, pay for my mother's care in hospice, and get my brother off methamphetamines, yes, you can help."

Harp was himself recovering from catastrophic events, but he was thoroughly impressed with how bad her situation was. He lamely offered, "Would money help some?"

"Money would help lots, Mr. Harper, but it wouldn't get my job back, or my house sold, or keep my stupid meth-head brother from stealing anything he can find," she laughed again and continued, "including my damned wrist watch."

Harp winced as she then started crying. But a thought came to him. He could do something, he realized. "Selling your house would take care of part of it, wouldn't it?"

"Yes, I had planned that half the money from the sale would take care of Mom at least for a couple of years. Why do you ask, Mr. Harper? Are you planning to move to Muncie, Indiana?" Again, the bitter laugh.

"Half the money?"

"My brother Donald owns half."

"Luna, I have lots of money. Yes, I can buy your house so you will have money in the bank. No, I am not planning on moving to Muncie. Who are you listed with?"

With a note of hope in her voice, she gave Harp information on the listing. "Okay, I'll call you back in a couple of days. Hang in there. I want to help."

In two days, with Kip's help through his own huge property management firm, Luna Norse's house in Muncie had been bought by an anonymous buyer for the listed price. Checks were immediately provided to Luna and her brother who emphatically agreed that neither ever wanted to see the other again. She would spend her portion on her mother's care. He would spend his on ever increasing amounts of meth and would die from an overdose of fentanyl within six months. Harp would repay Kip. He planned to turn the house back over to Luna in payment for the information he hoped she could provide.

Harp called again a week after the sale. "Oh, God, Mr. Harper, I don't know how you did it, but you cannot imagine how much you have helped us. I have set up an account for Mom's care and have enough left over to carry me until I find work. Thank you, thank you." She cried again, but this time it was in relief.

"Luna, I am glad I could help. Now I need your help." Harp had decided not to beat around the bush. "You remember what we talked about before? You related a whole lot of stuff about the Donettis. I need to know more."

Harp waited out the silence on the other end. Then, with some suspicion, "Why?"

"The simple answer is to survive. Arturo is still determined to get me. He has now tried twice and has almost succeeded." Harp would not yet reveal to her his intent to do more than protect himself. "I would like you to come here and spend a few days. I hope to learn enough to be prepared for whatever he's going to do." Harp would later apologize for this lie. Right now he couldn't scare her off.

"Come there?"

"I'll explain later, but it's really not a good time for me to travel."

"Where are you?"

"Let's just say I'm hiding out in Pennsylvania."

"I'm sorry, Mr. Harper, but I just can't picture you hiding from anyone or anything."

"That's true usually, but, for the moment, I am recuperating."

"Recuperating from what?"

"Two gunshot wounds to the head." He had decided to move the conversation along a little more quickly. He heard the phone clatter as if it had been dropped.

There was clicking and a rustle while her phone was being brought back to her ear. He could hear her breathing heavily. Finally, "Did he do it?"

"He had it done. Yes."

"What about the police. Can't they protect you?"

"No, they can't have someone sitting on my doorstep forever. They know about this, and they want to get him, too. But, he's in Italy. He's got others to do his dirty work. It could happen any-time, anywhere. Nobody knows how many people he can bring to the job."

"And you are hiding from his people now?"

"Correct."

"Well, how long can you hide? I mean, you have to have a life."

"I intend to."

She answered, speaking slowly as if thinking while talking. "That means you've only got three ways to go: fight, hide, or die."

"That's right." Harp was impressed at her quickness.

"And you want my help to get this monster before he gets you." There was a different, flatter tone to her voice. It sounded like she was about to say no.

"Yes."

"And you think I know things that might help you do this."

"Yes."

"How do I get there?" The abruptness of the decision almost caught Harp off guard. This time her voice was pure steel.

He acted as though this had been expected. "I'll give you detailed instructions. I suggest you fly in. You will be picked up at the airport and brought here."

"I'll be staying in the same place as you?" It was a question somehow full of meaning.

Harp could be dense sometimes, but he did pick up on the real question. "This is a very large protected suite with plenty of room for two people. You will have your own room and bath. You have my word that I will not do anything to offend you. From what you told me earlier, your experiences with some men would make you suspicious and I respect that."

She was quietly appreciative of this acknowledgement and asked, "How long would I stay?"

"As long or as short a stay as you decide. A few days at least, probably."

After a thoughtful silence, Norse said, "I'll have to see to the contents of my house first. That will take a while."

"Leave it as it is. You will have plenty of time to take care of that when you get back. I need you here." Harp thought it might just be too pat to now say that she was going to keep the house.

After another long silence, she said, "I'll let you know my arrival time."

With a great sense of relief, Harp said, "We'll be there." He gave directions for her to follow to the pickup point.

19

Thinking that Norse might be reluctant to travel with Kip, whom she did not know, Harp felt he should be there when Luna arrived. Kip drove to the airport while Harp rode slumped mostly out of sight in the back seat. He was wearing clothes Kip had bought at his direction. He had given Kip his old measurements and, for now, everything seemed to be too large. They were parked in the passenger pickup area when he saw her exit the building. She spotted the sign Kip was holding and gracefully strode toward the car dragging a large wheeled suitcase. She was more attractive than he remembered. She was tall, slender, and had an attractive face with a high forehead over hazel eyes, small nose, and a sensual lower lip with the permanent pucker with which some women are blessed. She wore different, more stylish glasses and had little to no makeup other than light lipstick. Her light brown hair was in its usual tight bun in the back. She wore a dated but classic straight brown skirt with tweed jacket over a pale-yellow sweater and low, very sensible brown shoes. She seemed fit and confident.

Harp watched as she shook hands with Kip and followed him to the rear door opposite Harp. She smoothly slid into the seat and Kip closed her door. She turned to fasten her seat belt and saw Harp. Her eyes widened–followed by a sharp intake of breath at his appearance. With both hands covering her mouth and head shaking slowly, she tried to process the change in this intensely vital man she remembered. Harp appeared to be a bundle of clothes slouched against the door. Pants, shirt, jacket, all were too large. He was wearing a knitted cap that did not totally cover the dressing still necessary on the forehead wound. His beard was a month old. His eyes were not the same, either. They were just as direct but looked somehow very tired.

Harp smiled and said, "I feel a lot better than I look."

Norse sighed in relief. "Boy, I hope so. You look terrible." She studied his face a bit more and said, "I can't believe that they would do this to you."

Harp laughed, "Well, this is sure as hell a lot better than dying, which is what they intended."

Kip interrupted, asking Norse, "Is that everything? We ready to go?"

Norse said yes and Harp said, "Let's go." He went on to introduce Kip. "Luna Norse, this is Wellington Kipling Finch-Smithers IV. We call him Kip."

Kip quickly explained, "Actually, Sarge came up with that name because when we met he couldn't even remember my name. I'm surprised he can say it today." They laughed.

Harp complimented Kip by saying, "Kip was a good soldier who had been wounded real bad before we first met. He became a key member of our small team and was right there through the worst of it. I'm really proud of this guy." He reached up and hit Kip on the shoulder. Kip looked up at the rear-view mirror and smiled.

Norse watched the interplay and recognized the comradery they shared. It made her feel more certain that she was in good hands.

Harp continued. "We will be staying at a place that Kip owns for the time being. I need some more time to totally recover, and I can use that time to debrief you, sorry, to get from you all the information I can about the Donettis."

Norse winced and shuddered at the mention of that name.

"Right now, the three of us in this car are the only people who know where I am. I don't like it, but it's probably necessary. We have to assume that they have people looking for me. Maybe now more than ever." Harp shifted position and carefully scratched the scar on the back of his head. "I will explain in detail what I hope to do when we are alone at the apartment. Kip will know nothing of what we talk about to preserve his deniability."

Kip said over his shoulder, "Hey, Sarge, you know I will back you whatever."

"Sure, Kip. I know that. But this is my choice, so follow orders." Kip shrugged.

Norse asked, more out of curiosity than fear, "What about my deniability? To be frank, this all sounds particularly grim."

"The plan is that you will be back in Muncie well before anything happens. Hopefully, no one will even know that you've been here. There should be no connection."

Norse nodded thoughtfully. "Okay."

Harp suddenly asked, "Do you have a cell phone?"

"Of course. Why?"

"Have you made any calls since you got here?"

Norse, puzzled, said, "No. Why?"

"Because we need to be very sure that your location is not known. I want you to take the battery out of your phone now. Okay?"

"I don't know how to do that," Norse replied, slightly annoyed. She handed the phone to Harp who quickly removed the battery and handed it back. She put phone and battery in her purse.

After he had removed the battery, Harp smiled in an effort to placate an annoyed Luna. "The way technology has advanced, the bad guys can tell where you are, who you talked to, how long you talked, and what you were wearing when you dialed." Her head came around at the last detail. "Just kidding about the last one." What Harp didn't explain was that he had taken part in many operations where the person making the call was targeted and executed using this very technology.

20

Harp woke up to the very pleasant smell of breakfast cooking. After Kip had dropped them off back at the suite and Harp had shown Norse where her quarters were, Harp had gone to bed. He now had a regulation extra-large shower cap so he could enjoy a long hot shower. Refreshed and dressed, he went to the kitchen to find that Norse had cooked eggs, potatoes, bacon, and toast. It wasn't until he had eaten about everything on the table that he realized he had probably taken a big portion of her share.

She had been watching him as he ate. She sipped her coffee and studied the wounds and scars, which were now shown in much better light. She was appalled at what had been done to him and impressed that he had not only survived but was now sitting across from her with a ravenous appetite. It was very apparent that he was not going to just survive, but do it in a robust manner.

Harp apologized. "Sorry, I can't remember the last time I sat down to a home-cooked breakfast that I didn't cook. I totally pigged out. I can fix some more if you're still hungry."

Norse laughed. "No, I've had plenty. Besides, I haven't had the pleasure of watching a man eat my cooking in a long, long time." She stood up, "Let me get you some more coffee."

Harp watched as she very gracefully arose from the chair and walked to the coffee machine. He could not help but observe the dancer's grace with which she moved. She was wearing her usual straight skirt with a long-sleeved sweater but was now wearing off-white sneakers. Her glasses were hooked into the top of her sweater. Harp thought that it was funny how some little thing like that can make a woman look bookish. With her hair in its usual bun, she looked how he thought a teacher or librarian would look.

She brought his coffee and watched as he enjoyed the brew and finished the last piece of toast. Norse was apparently comfortable being here in this new environment with a man she barely knew. Harp swore to himself again that he would never do anything to change that.

With no preamble, she asked, "Do you know what an eidetic memory is?"

"No. Is that like a photographic memory?"

"Yes and no. There is some evidence that they are different types of memory and that they occur in response to different stimuli." She sipped. "There are some studies showing that eidetic memory will, in many cases, become photogenic, or photographic, memories."

Harp nodded, not knowing where this was going.

"I have what I think is eidetic memory. It is the type that allows a person to recall in minute detail everything that the eye and ear perceives. With me, these images are immediately transferred into what I think of as my photographic memory,"

Norse paused, took a deep breath, and continued, "whether or not I wish them to be."

With eyes closed, she continued, "For example, if I live to be ninety, I will remember in finite detail the picture of you sitting there, what you are wearing, those scars, the scars on your knuckles, the mole on your forearm, everything. And, that will include everything that you say and do." She shrugged and chuckled. "That is my curse, or blessing, depending on how you use it."

She sat with eyes closed, obviously trying to prepare herself. Harp was shocked to see tears forming in the corners of her eyes. She quickly brushed them away and turned to face Harp squarely. She had made up her mind to proceed. Norse was suddenly transformed from a pleasant breakfast companion into an impassioned woman. She clenched the edge of the table in front of her and, with white knuckles, leaned toward Harp and ground out the words in a harsh whisper through white lips, "Mr. Harper, I *know* what you need. I *know* where you want to take me. And, yes, I remember everything. I remember every damned, painful, tortuous, thing that I felt and heard there. And what you want will require me to dig them up, drag them out, then feel them and see them all over again! I can't go to any part of it without going to the last part first!" She was now almost shouting. "And you know what they did!" She abruptly twisted up and out of her chair.

Harp visibly recoiled at her intensity. He sat back now, suddenly doubtful that he had done the right thing in bringing Norse into his plan. "Jesus, Luna, I just didn't think, I didn't have any idea, that this would affect you this way." Shaking his head, he waved his arms, crossing palms down as if to put a stop to the whole thing. "Let's just forget it. I'm sorry I did this. Go home and get on with your life."

Norse laughed bitterly. "Get on with my life? Are you kidding me? I can't ever get on with my life until I do just what you want me to do!" She sat again and leaned forward, elbows on the table, and said more calmly, "I have to do this. What you do not yet realize is that you are my last, best hope. I have not been with a man since that time. I need to live again, like a normal woman. Do you understand?"

Harp listened just as intensely as Norse spoke. And then he did understand. He said with a note of wonder, "You have to do the same thing I do." He then modified that. "You *want* to do the thing that I am going to do."

Norse sat with her head down and nodded in small jerky movements. "I don't have any more choice than you do," she mumbled. She raised her head and looked into Harp's eyes. "I want my life back. I want to live, to love, to laugh, without this stinking weight on my heart. I want my mind to be clear. The death of his son was only a beginning. The death of the father will set me free. I will do anything to see that happen. He wants to kill you. He has already killed me. Do you understand now?"

Harp, still stunned at her passion, nodded, "Yes."

Norse smiled grimly. "Good. Let's get started."

Harp smiled, "Do you think we could finish our coffee and get comfortable first?"

Norse laughed and relaxed just a bit. They moved to the living area, each with a coffee in hand. Harp sat on the sofa, feet up, waiting.

Norse sat but, as she began to talk, she paced. Sometimes she was consumed with rage. Sometimes she was overcome by sadness and cried. At first, her memories were scattered, ranked by intensity. Harp suggested that she begin again, this time relating events chronologically. She talked for hours. This was just the first session. She provided incredible details about the times she spent with Dominic. Harp was astonished at her recall. She remembered everything Dominic had ever said to her. She remembered every place he had taken her. She remembered even the subtle hints at places and activities relating to the Donettis' crooked empire.

For two days, Harp listened. He listened as he would have if this were a briefing on a mission where casualties could be expected—where he knew that listening could mean the difference between life and death. Which, as it turned out, was exactly the case. Even with his prodigious memory for detail, Harp realized this stuff would have to be organized into an eventual action plan. She had no concept of a tactical application of her knowledge. It was a stream of consciousness exercise for her—even perhaps a sort of cleansing. Harp listened and plucked salient potentials from her narrative as she talked. He did not interrupt. He took notes. He was preparing for an old battle strategy: If you know you are going to be attacked, you attack first.

21

From Norse's recollections, it became obvious that Dominic's duties, as the son of the boss, were mainly as a courier, a glorified deliveryman. What he delivered was money. His belief that Norse was totally enraptured with his charms allowed him to rationalize taking Norse with him in the conduct of these duties—sometime even during a date. Their dates were almost always on weekends, and that was when he did the pickups. Norse would wait in the large black Mercedes SUV while Dominic would enter central collection points around the city and return with valises, satchels, or even paper bags, which he would throw into the back seat. Some were quite large. At the beginning, Norse asked what was in those bags. Dominic would only grin and say, "Our future." But she soon knew it was money and, to her eventual shame, was impressed.

Norse interrupted the flow of her recollections to note that it was ironic that he died during one of the few times he tried to assume the tougher job of enforcer because he was trying to please his father. She resumed. At a prearranged meeting spot, he would park next to another black SUV into which all the bags would then be transferred. She asked one time where it all went. Dominic laughed and said, "To the 'bank,'" and made air quotes with his fingers. Norse remembered the location where the money was transferred.

Norse remembered everything. Everywhere. There was one particular instance, however, where even in her merely curious innocence, she noticed a tension in Dominic's behavior that might have been taken as fear. Once, he got a phone call while they were on their way to dinner. Dominic said only, "They all there?" and nodded. Then they stopped outside a small restaurant on the corner of a quiet street near the waterfront. The restaurant had no signage other than "Pasta Calamarata" on the glass over the door. It was late. There was a "closed" sign hanging crookedly inside the door glass. Dominic reached behind the seat for a small cloth grocery bag and mumbled nervously, "Gotta make the Sunday delivery."

It was a small place that seemed empty except for an aged bartender sitting on a cooler watching the TV over the bar. This time, Dominic was carrying money *in* instead of bringing it out as usual. She watched as Dominic entered the unlocked front door and walked through the tables straight to the back and knocked on the door. The bartender seemed intent to not look at him as he passed by in either direction. The door was opened then quickly closed after he entered. In the brief time the door was open, she saw two faces looking at Dominic. He came out empty-handed in just a little over a minute. Even as he walked through the restaurant, Norse sensed that his demeanor was different. It appeared as though he wanted to hurry but made himself walk steadily to the exit. He jumped in the car and they sped away.

Norse was moved to ask, "What's wrong? What happened in there?"

Dominic shook his head and was slow to answer. "Nothing." He then added. "Those guys give me the creeps."

"Why?" She was surprised to see this reaction in him.

He gave it some thought. "You know, in this business, I see everything. I see all kinds of guys who have done just about everything. I kinda get used to it because they don't bother with me and I don't bother with them. Most of them are real dumbasses who would do anything for a buck. We pay them as long as they do as they're told and kick 'em out if they don't."

"So, how are these men different?"

"These guys...these guys are not human like you and me." Dominic thought some more. "We operate in a tough world, you know, where bad things happen to people. But these guys, these guys will ice a person just because they feel like it." Dominic nodded to himself as if in confirmation, "And I know they would do me, even me, if they felt like it." He shuddered.

Norse was puzzled. "Then why do you associate with people like that?"

"They're kind of like protection for the family. If we get threats, which happens in our business, these guys take care of it. They remove the threats—and they have removed lots of threats, if you know what I mean. They're specialists. Everybody needs specialists." He turned to look at Norse and roughly said, "Let's not talk about it anymore. Forget you were ever there." Which of course, for Norse, meant that she would never forget.

There was another pickup that stood out in Norse's memory. It was another of those innocuous storefronts with nothing special advertised. This one was different in that, during the day, there was a steady stream of people entering and leaving the establishment. Dominic arrived back at the truck with an especially large and heavy canvas bag, and he was grinning.

"The ol' man's going to love this one," he said.

"Why? What's that place?"

"That, my dear, is our most successful betting parlor. The odds favored us today, and we made a bundle."

"I thought betting was legal in New Jersey. Why do it in a spot like this?"

Dominic laughed, "It is legal, but when you win with us, nobody knows you made some money."

"You mean the IRS doesn't know about it," Norse concluded. He grinned and nodded.

Harp was getting an idea of the big picture. He was trying to put all this information into a logical approach. The goal was still to get Arturo Donetti before he got Harp. Harp believed that the only way to get to Donetti was to hurt his organization. But he was one guy. How could he hit Donetti hard enough to bring him out into the open where Harp could employ his special skills?

Luna Norse wasn't done. "Oh yes, there was one other curious stop. It was on a Sunday morning, and he was taking me back to the studio so I could catch up on some paperwork. We stopped right outside this little shop in a strip mall. The sign said 'Bathroom Supplies Tubs and Tiles.' Dominic had a key for the outer door. He went right to a door behind the counter. This door had a keypad. He thought I couldn't see what he punched in, but I saw two numbers top left, one number left middle and one right middle, and one number bottom right, and the zero."

Harp said, "Let's see. That would be 124690."

Norse nodded and continued. "He came out carrying a gun

case for a long gun. He put it in the back and said he was going hunting and winked. Now, I grew up in the country, so I know a damn rifle case when I see one. It has the special area built in for the scope, so I know it wasn't a shotgun."

Harp was excited by this news. Could this be the place where the Donetti mob kept its arsenal? He had been trying to figure out how he was going to secure weapons to carry out his plan. This could be the answer. Plus, the irony pleased him. Get Arty with his own guns.

Norse had been pacing as she talked. She was wearing the usual skirt and sweater. After that last bit of information, she paused, then said, "I think that's it." She flopped on the sofa, threw her feet up, and laid her head back on a cushion. "Now what?" But she hadn't told Harp everything. There were still memories too painful to relate. She had decided to keep them to herself for now. Maybe she would find a way to erase these memories on her own.

"Now I'll try to take all these pieces and put together a plan. The number one objective is to come out of this alive." He smiled and added, "Number two is to make sure Arty doesn't." Harp stood up stiffly. He had been sitting all day thinking and writing. "Meanwhile, I'm beat. I'm hitting the sack."

"Let me check the dressings. It's been all day." Harp scowled and sat back down.

Norse gently checked for signs of infection and found none. She was amazed that he had survived such horrendous wounds. She moved his head around during her examination and, when she was done, resisted the urge to pull it against her breast. It had been years since she had been held, years since she had held a man.

Knowing nothing of her thoughts, Harp got up again and walked toward his bedroom.

Norse said, "I'm tired too." But she paused and watched as he walked away. She raised a hand and opened her mouth but said nothing as he entered his bedroom and closed the door. He had made a promise, and he would keep it. She was sure that she wanted him to. She was very sure, she told herself as she went to her room alone.

22

Luna Norse finished her jog around the strip mall on the out-skirts of Trenton. She was wearing typical jogging clothes plus earphones, sunglasses, and a visor. She looked no different than the other hundreds of women seen jogging everywhere every day. After making a big loop of the entire mall, she ran to Harp's car waiting among the other cars in the large parking area. It was parked where Harp could see the front of the business calling itself Bathroom Supplies Tubs and Tiles and the other shops on either side. Harp was pleased to note that Norse was not winded from her run.

She was breathing evenly as she reported. "The back door is metal with no handle. There is a light over the door but I couldn't see any cameras. There is nothing to block a car driving away in either direction. On the other side of the alley is a chain link fence grown up with weeds." Harp made a conscious effort not to look at her bare legs and running bra as she spoke.

Then Harp reported, "It looks like Sunday would be best. I haven't seen anyone going into the businesses on either side. The front door is the kind set in an aluminum frame, which I know from experience can be bent out of the way with a large enough crowbar. We can get in easy enough. We just have to hope that the combination for the inside door is right."

Norse nodded and asked, "What about alarms and cameras inside?"

"If this is what we think it is, I don't see how they want to bring the cops down on the place. I'm guessing there's no typical alarms. Cameras? I don't know. That's so easy anymore. They could be sitting in Seattle watching monitors right now. I think we have to assume it's being watched inside. As far as that goes, we have to assume that we're being watched all the time." Harp was very familiar with the work done by satellites, drones, and spy planes.

"Which means?" Norse asked as they were driving away, heading back to Philadelphia.

"It means we have to get in and get out fast. We know *something* is in there. I should be able to tell pretty quick what we've got. It means we can never appear to be who we actually are." He smiled at Norse and asked, "You still game for this?"

"Definitely. We go." She laughed at her own audacity. Harp carefully patted her on her shoulder.

Harp was pleased that she was still with him in this. He knew he could not do this alone. As he drove the thirty-some miles back to their apartment, he revisited his logic. Harp had concluded that he could not get to Donetti without weapons. All he had was the thirty-eight that he started with weeks ago. He thought about going to that storage unit and getting that damned foot locker, but he knew that the whole area was covered with lights and cameras. He wanted to stay gone, maybe dead, for as long as he could.

This was just the first volley in Harp's war. He hoped for Norse's sake it would work. It was the setup for the next volley.

The following Sunday at 5:45 a.m., a man wearing a motorcycle helmet stepped from a black rental Toyota Camry and quickly strode to the door of the store known as Bathroom Supplies Tub and Tiles. The Camry drove off. Taking a long crowbar from where he had been carrying it close to his leg, he jammed it between the door and the frame. The latch was easily disabled, and he walked directly to the door of the inside room. The first try at the combination lock didn't work. Harp tried again and it clicked. He opened the door, closed it, and hit the light switch. He was mildly shocked to find that it was not an arsenal, but a working gunsmith's shop. Apparently, this was the gun shop for the mob. At separate areas around the room were the lathe, milling machine, grinder, polisher, various hand tools, and an arc welder. From the parts visible, it looked like a large part of the work was installing silencers and otherwise altering all kinds of firearms. Probably a lot of it was removing serial numbers.

Harp went directly to the back door to find that it had a slide bolt and keyed lock but none of the alarms usually found on the inside of such doors. Rather than looking for the key, Harp easily found a shotgun and shells. He loaded the automatic twelve gauge with deer slugs. He was very familiar with this model with the extended tube, which was in common use in the Army. Without pausing, Harp shot the lock twice in rapid succession and the door swung open. Norse, also wearing a motorcycle helmet stepped through the door. They had anticipated this would be necessary, so she was waiting well away from the door. Still, she was shaken when the slugs blasted through the door with pieces of insulation and metal flying outward. She hesitantly entered and watched Harp for instructions.

Harp was right, there were no alarms, but there were cameras, and these cameras relayed all their actions to a private security firm operating out of the Bronx. This firm promptly called the assigned number, which resulted in another black SUV speeding to the indicated location. It was very close and took only minutes to get there. Once again, the training and experiences of ordinary civilian killers and hoodlums did not prepare them for a confrontation with an experienced battle-hardened veteran.

Harp and Norse both heard the buzz that indicated someone had entered the outside shop; they both heard the clicking of the combination lock at the second door. Harp dropped to his knee and waited. Norse dove behind some wooden crates. The three Donetti men punched the numbers on the lock. They had decided on a full-frontal attack. They jerked the door open and rushed into the shop shooting. Harp was ready. He had done this before, but not in civilian life. They had a moment to digest the image of a person in a helmet kneeling with a shotgun pointing at their noses. Then the shotgun fired three times and the three went down. Two were killed outright. The third was wearing a vest and was knocked unconscious by the force of the slug hitting over his heart.

Harp waved at Norse to get up and come toward him. He motioned with a finger to his mouth to remain silent. She nodded. He pointed all around the room and at her, making a strange motion with his hand and forefinger. She nodded again and removed a can of wasp spray from her shoulder bag. It was the only thing easily available they could think of with a long spray. Norse found each of the cameras and sprayed them so no more of their actions would be clearly visible on camera. They still had said nothing.

Harp selected a large canvas bag and began filling it with

things he thought might be needed. He first took four pistols of various calibers, two silencers, the shotgun, a military rifle, a silenced rifle with a scope, a good supply of ammo for all, and two vests. The rifle had a tag that said only *ready*. Now knowing what the business was, he started opening drawers. There was a drawer with ten more pistols waiting for modification. They had to have a history. He threw five of them in the bag. He wanted one more thing, but they were running out of time. Just as he was about to quit looking, he found it in a metal cabinet: a small box with the *Danger Explosives* warning logo.

He tucked it under one arm and picked up the duffle bag with the other and was approaching the door when he heard a shot behind him. Harp clumsily turned with his arms full to see Norse standing over the third victim of Harp's shooting. He had regained consciousness and was moving his hand toward one of the pistols lying on the floor when Norse shot him in the temple. Harp had given her the old thirty-eight just in case. He never dreamed that she would have to use it. She seemed to be frozen, standing over her victim, gun still pointing downward.

Norse said something in a strange garbled language and followed him to the door. Harp carefully placed the explosives in the trunk and threw the duffle bag into the back seat. Norse ran around to the driver's seat and started the engine. Harp leaned into the car and whispered for her to wait. He went back inside for a moment and returned. When he got back, he saw that Norse had already started to change from a helmeted female to an elderly woman with long gray hair, thick glasses, and cheap pink coat. As she slowly drove out of the alley, Harp became an old man with a gray beard, thick glasses, and stupid hat. While they waited at the stop light leaving the shopping area, three more black vehicles roared past them heading toward the scene.

"They are not cops," Norse observed.

"Nope, I doubt the police will ever get to see what happened." He put his head against the headrest and closed his eyes. He was troubled. Not by what he did, but what she did. "Luna, I really never figured you would get in this deep. You didn't need to do that. I should've."

"You had your hands full. Your back was turned." She thought for a moment. "My grandfather was Norwegian and had a saying." Norse quoted her grandfather.

"Is that what you said in there?"

"Yes. It means that if you want to eat a deer roast, you have to kill the deer."

23

Harp and Norse transferred their take to Harp's Ford and drove the Camry back to the car rental shack in Philly and left it there with the keys under the floor mat. Everything was soon taken up to the suite. Harp then made an important phone call. "Kip, you need to be gone for a while. Someplace where a lot of people know you and can see you."

Kip understood. "It's started then."

"Yes. We are active. I'll let you know when we leave. Right now, I don't think we've left any tracks, so you're clear. Let's keep it that way."

"Okay. Good luck. You know I'm with you."

"I know. Thanks for everything. I'll see you again someday, I hope." Harp disconnected with deep regret over the way the fates were isolating him from his friends. He removed the battery and SIM card from the phone. He twisted and flushed the SIM card.

Norse was listening. "Let me ask you something, Harp. Would that guy have shot me or you if he could have?"

"Luna, he would have shot either of us without a minute's

hesitation. That's his job. What you did probably saved both our lives."

She considered this and said, "Well, okay then." She pulled off the wig and threw it on the counter, "I need a long hot shower. See you later." She was shaken but being brave. Harp appreciated what she was going through. The first time a human kills a human was often very difficult for the killer to assimilate.

There was a concentrated effort on the part of Donetti's crew to sanitize the place. Within twenty-four hours, the bodies were gone, the machinery was gone, the doors were repaired, and there was a sign on the door saying simply "Gone Out of Business." The effect, however, was deep and long-lasting. Adding to the breadth of the problem for the mob was what Harp had written on one of the walls. It said only *NY Calling!* written with a big felt tip pen. That, by itself, was enough to put heavy guards out for every Donetti-controlled establishment—and even some of their homes. They would send emissaries to New York to very carefully ask around if anyone there knew of a problem with Trenton. It threatened to upset a carefully worked out balance among different territories. There was a new tension in all relationships in Trenton. New levels of distrust sprang up where old relationships had flourished. And yet, all of this had to happen without the involvement of the law. They could not complain about the shooting without explaining where and why it had happened.

The whole situation sent Arturo Donetti into paroxysms of rage. Still in Italy, he had a long list of questions. The biggest of course was *who!* After that was *how* and then *why?* Most enraging was the fact that the guy who broke in *knew the fucking combination!* Arty was extremely frustrated because he had to express everything over the goddamned phone. Arturo soon concluded that this had to be an inside job. Someone in one of his operations had told the thieves where all their gun work was done.

What he really missed was having his son present back in Trenton because his son was the only person he could totally trust when the shit came down. Thinking of this again reaffirmed his determination to get the fucker who had killed his son. Now, more than ever, he was determined that this scarafaggio Harper was going to die an ugly death. But, this most recent thing had to be resolved first.

Arturo's lawyers were ordered to study the tapes from the security company. They brought in an expert. The tapes told him a lot. They showed a man in an elaborate helmet coming through the door after punching in the combination. He then blew the back door lock out and another person entered from behind the building. This was obviously a woman. She was also wearing a helmet. They studied the contents of the gang's arsenal. They heard the buzzer. The man spun and dropped to a knee and waited. It only took seven seconds. He then fired three times hitting all three of Arty's men, who had stupidly rushed into the room. Then the woman sprayed the cameras with insect spray. It didn't actually block the lens but made the images from that point on so distorted as to be useless for identification purposes. The sound was still there. They listened as Harp and Norse searched the room and collected certain gear. Then there was the sound of gunfire. One bullet. Small caliber. Then, quite clearly, the woman said something in a foreign language. They left the room. A car trunk, then a car door, closed. The man came back in and did something and then left for good. A car door closed.

The motor started and they drove away. The next sound was of a large group of men rushing into the room and cursing.

The expert summarized: "You got a guy maybe six, six one, I'm guessing probably late thirties, early forties. He's healthy but actually kind of too thin for the height. The move he made to get those guys was not normal. I would say this guy is experienced military. He did not hesitate to shoot. He's done it before. You don't teach this stuff. You learn by doing. I think he's got a slight limp, right leg. Not sure about that. Also, he knew what he wanted and, from what you say, he left a lot behind. This was not about money. This guy wanted this stuff so he could use it. And, here's something you oughta be aware of. He took a whole bunch of those pistols that were there for cleaning. I would guess those particular pieces have a history. If they turn up on the street, say, as a throw-away, you could have another kind of problem. Because of the height on the wall, he's the one who left the message. Also, he took the TNT because he knows how to use it. Not many do."

He then switched to the woman. "The woman is some younger. She's about five eight, five nine, maybe 125 pounds. She's also got a helmet, but it's like she never wore one before because she keeps hitching at it. She's new at this. She came through the door scared but was okay when she got busy. She is smart. She wore gloves. They both wore gloves. She sprayed the cameras after he told her to. Now here's the interesting part: when your last guy got it in the head, even with the smeared lens, we could tell the guy is nowhere near your guy on the floor. That means *she* did him. Which means she can be cold, man. And, last but not least, she said something real clear after she offed him. It's the only thing anybody said. Something about heeyorts and heeyortskits. I think it's Scandinavian or something around there."

The lawyer summarized, "So we've got a professional soldier and foreign woman stealing certain weapons. How do we know these are not terrorists?"

The expert answered. "They ain't terrorists—but maybe worse. They took only what they needed. They took just a bag full of stuff. They left a lot. They took what they plan to use. If they use it, you got a shitstorm."

Harp was right. It was a long time before the police got word of what had happened and then it was the word of a snitch. The word that came down was that some radical rightist neo-Nazis from New York might have ripped off the Donetti mob and coldly iced three dudes in the process.

24

Arturo Donetti decided to embark on a two-pronged approach. He would continue efforts to solve the situation with the New York people, but he would also try a new approach to finding out what happened to Harper. His determination to get revenge was stronger than ever. He had the centuries-old tradition of *vendetta il onore* to uphold. This was the other prong.

Arturo was very intelligent. He knew that mob guys often looked like mob guys. They weren't known for finesse. He wanted a new approach to finding Harper. He had heard of this specialist who was very, very good at finding people and who had few qualms about why it was done—mostly because right after they were found, they were found dead. His name was Nolan Rast. He was a former New York City cop who was kicked off the force for taking bribes. These bribes were not doughnuts and coffee, but amounts high into the thousands for losing evidence, forgetting notes, corrupting crime scenes, and such. Finally, the proof of his deeds was irrefutable, and he was coldly dismissed with no benefits after 17 years on the force. The sad thing was, he had all the qualities to make a real good cop—except for honesty. He was smart, healthy, well-educated, strong, and intuitive.

Then, suddenly, he was broke and ready to do just about anything for money. So, he became a mob blood hound. Give him just a little scent of the prey and he would find him. When he found the prey, the next step was determined by how much money was offered. Arturo offered a half million at proof of termination. No matter who did it. Plus expenses.

An important thing Rast had going for himself was his appearance. He was of medium height, slender, and dressed well. He had curly red hair neatly kept over an open friendly face with a natural smile, small nose, good teeth, and bushy red eyebrows. People just naturally trusted him. When he went into the Battle, which was his starting point, Tommy was working. After he smiled and presented the card from a well-known insurance company, Tommy was anxious to tell what he knew. The bottom line was that Tommy did not know much but he was very worried about Harp. He hoped Rast would find Harp. The business was doing great, he reported, but there were some key decisions coming up and they needed the owner to be there. No, Tommy said, he did not know where Harp was or even if he was alive. He suggested that Rast talk to Detective Carroll or maybe to the guy who was with him in the hospital. You know, the guy with one foot, Marion Bondurant. "Hold on," he said. Tommy went back into the office and came out with a slip of paper with the address of the farm. "He had this pinned on the bulletin board in the office. I knew I seen it somewhere."

Rast decided that he would fly to North Carolina and talk to this farmer with one foot. He did not give any advance notice of his visit. Rast drove his rental car into the yard of a large, well-kept farm. He drove up a long, fenced drive past fields of crops, pasture, grazing cattle, and hay. He walked around the yard of the neat farmstead, looking at the house, the barns, garages, etc. Soon a pickup drove into the yard and a large solid looking man got out and walked toward Rast with a smile. He strode directly to Rast with hand out.

"Hey, how you doin'?" he said, with a smile.

"I'm doing great." Rast responded. "I was just appreciating what a fine operation you have here."

"Why, thank you, Mr. ... ?"

"Name is Peterson."

"Okay, Mr. Peterson, how can I help you?" Bonny took a large handkerchief from his pocket and wiped his face, waiting.

"I'm with Large Cap Insurance and we have claims to settle with ..." Rast pretended to look at his notes, "a Mr. Horace B. Harper. It was suggested that you might be able to tell us where we can find this gentleman."

"Sure, sure," Bonny replied. "Let's go up and sit on the porch. Would you like some iced tea?" They walked up to the porch where Bonny directed Rast to a comfortable rocker. "I'll get us some tea and be right back." He went inside. Rast, feeling this was going to be easy, waited contentedly.

Bonny appeared after several minutes carrying two glasses of iced tea and put one on the table next to Rast. Rast was from New York, he hated iced tea, but sipped appreciatively.

"Now, Mr. Peterson, what was it that you needed to know?" Bonny asked, but there seemed to be a new level of tension in those words. He sat facing Rast.

"Mr. Harper carried a policy with our company for which the premium is long past due, and it will be canceled without immediate payment."

"Where are you located, Mr. Peterson?"

"Uh, our offices are in New York City."

"And you came all the way down here just to collect a payment on an insurance policy?" This time there was no mistaking the tone. "How much is this payment? He was an old friend. I'll just go ahead and make the payment for him."

"Uh, I don't know if that's permissible." Rast stood up. He decided that his bullshit wasn't working. It was time to get tough with this yokel. He pointed his finger at Bonny. "Look buddy, we're not messing around. We need to find Harper and, if you know where he is, it is important that you tell us."

Bonny remained sitting in his rocker, smiling with legs crossed, metal shin showing. "You know, Peterson, we were told that someone would come with a line of bullshit trying to trick us simple rural folks to rat out our old friend. What they didn't tell us was that this someone was an idiot." Bonny coldly looked into Rast's eyes and asked. "What do you think, Weeks, is this guy on the level?"

Rast spun around to find Phil Weeks, Bonny's partner, standing with a stainless Colt nine aimed right at his nose. "I don't know, Bonny. I'm picking up a smell here." He loudly sniffed the air once, then again. "Yup, I was right. That is the smell of shit. I believe it is Trenton, New Jersey, shit."

Bonny stepped up to Rast. He was no longer the friendly host. His voice had gone flat. "Don't move a muscle, Peterson. We've got about a thousand acres to bury you in. And, right now we are very close to doing it."

Rast was smart enough to be scared. He stood with his back to Bonny. He had never encountered such casual disregard for his threats. It did occur to him that nobody knew he was here. They could do it. They could bury him out here in the sticks and no one would know. He remained motionless as Bonny thoroughly searched his body just as he had a hundred times while searching robe-wearing enemies in the sandpit. Bonny quickly found his wallet–which was full of fake Peterson ID. He kept his wallet and phone.

But Bonny wasn't done. He told Rast to sit back down. "Keep an eye on him. I'm going to check the car." Bonny found a very expensive leather carry-on with many zippers and pockets in the back seat. He searched through all the compartments, found nothing, and was putting the bag back in the car. Rast was beginning to relax.

Weeks said, "Wait a minute, Bonny. Remember we saw one like this when we were checking people coming back into Ryad. It had a real tricky fake bottom that was hook-looped so strong we could hardly open it." Bonny snapped his fingers and nodded as he remembered and, holding the bag tightly, pulled hard on the rolled edge of the bottom, which appeared to be sewn in place. Rast thought, oh shit. The opened compartment revealed Rast's real wallet, credit cards in different names, including his own, a checkbook, and the information about their farm.

Rast leaped to his feet only to receive an expert chop to the base of the neck with the gun barrel. He dropped like a rock and stayed out. "What are we going to do with this guy?" Bonny asked.

"If anybody knows he was coming here, we can't do anything, uh, permanent," Weeks said.

Bonny grinned. "But we sure can make him sorry he ever came."

They devised a pretty wicked plan on the spot. "Let me have one of his credit cards. We got his address on the driver's license.

Why don't we have some stuff ordered and delivered there?" Weeks took the phone and the card and ordered several items of bomb making equipment charged to Rast's card to be delivered at Rast's address. "This should get the attention of the Feds. They're really sensitive to this kind of shit these days."

Next, Weeks took all the cards and got back on the phone. He was very good at manipulating these new cell phones. He was looking at the phone and laughing while Bonny watched. "Okay, now I just canceled all of his credit cards, even the Peterson cards. Now, all we got left to fix is his checkbook." Bonny nodded and removed a large set of wire cutters from his belt and neatly clipped a V-shape out of the routing number on the checks and deposit slips.

Bonny laughed. He had an idea. "What's that stuff you were using the other day to repair that canvas equipment cover? Some kind of super glue?"

"That stuff was terrible to work with. It sets so quick you have to move real fast not to screw it up." He thought he knew what his longtime partner was thinking. "I'll go get it."

Rast was still out when they set him back in the driver's seat of his rental. They were careful to lift him in and center him in the seat. He would not know until he tried to exit the car that his jacket and pants were immediately bonded to the fabric of the driver's seat.

Rast regained consciousness while sitting in his car. Bonny and Weeks were standing outside the open door smiling. Bonny was holding the keys. They watched as Rast rubbed his neck and slowly became fully aware of his situation. He looked at Weeks and said, "You fucker. You sucker punched me."

With a cool grin, Weeks said, "You don't know the half of it,

Mr. Nolan Rast. I would have done a lot more if I thought we could get away with it."

Bonny leaned in with one elbow on the roof and one on the edge of the car door. "You are a lucky man, Rast. We don't even know how many vermin worse than you we have killed. You get to drive out of here alive." He reached in and cruelly twisted Rast's ear. "Now, I want you to listen. You tell that Italian fuck Donetti to back off and leave all of us alone. That's all we want. He gave another twist. "And that means *all* of us." He let go of Rast's ear and stood back with a malicious grin. "And, you want to know what's really funny, Rast? The truth is that *we don't know* where Harper is. We don't even know if he is alive. This whole trip of yours was wasted from the git go." He handed Rast the keys and stood back.

Rast was profoundly shocked. He believed him. It was a co-lossal waste in so many ways. For all the time in his long career in law enforcement and then in this man tracking business, he was never so glad to get out of a situation as he was now.

But then, he did not yet know of the situation he would find himself in when he drove into the rental return at the air-port. The bright young lady with the clipboard walked up to his car and waited as he shut off the motor and opened the door. Her smile became strained as she watched Rast repeatedly go through the motions of swinging out of the seat only to find he couldn't move. There was something wrong. Rast finally looked down at the fabric between his legs and saw the sticky stuff. He started pulling at the cloth of his pants and jacket while cursing loudly and profanely and calling someone names. The shocked and frightened young lady left and brought back an airport cop. He didn't help by standing there and laughing. He called some more cops who all watched as Rast wiggled out of his jacket, then slid upward and out of his pants. The rental firm supervisor was there by now. He explained that Rast would have to pay for the cost of replacing the seat. Rast, standing in the airport indoor parking garage in socks, tighty-whities, shirt, and tie, in front of a group of laughing policemen, agreed in desperation — only to find that his credit cards had all been cancelled and he only had a few bucks cash.

The rental supervisor pressed charges, and the mirthful cops took a nearly apoplectic Rast to the local jail. At least at the jail, he was given pants to wear. He was finally bonded out via the internet by his laughing lawyer who knew he was good for the money.

Bonny texted Carroll to thank him for the earlier heads up and told him everything that had happened. It wasn't his state, so Carroll overlooked the possible illegalities of their actions and expressed appreciation for the information. This put Mr. Nolan Rast on police radar everywhere as a possible hit man for the Donettis. Carroll asked if Bonny had anything new on Harper. The answer was the same as always. Nobody knew anything. Harp had disappeared. Maybe he was dead. Carroll believed Bondurant but felt in his bones that Harper was out there and something was about to happen.

25

Harp had decided that the next action would be to take some of the Donetti money. He and Norse focused on the events of the day that Dominic had picked up collections from several locations and then delivered the take to a certain point. Norse was able to recreate the route they had taken and the spot where the transfer had been made. She remembered it was early on a Saturday evening and Dominic's pickups were simple affairs where he would park next to a vehicle in a large parking lot and punch the button opening the rear hatch. Without saying anything, someone would get out of the other car and throw bags into the back of Dominic's SUV. Dominic would close the hatch and they would drive off. No one said a word during the process. When all the stops had been made, the back of the truck was piled high. Dominic would drive to the parking deck on Main, go to the open fourth floor of the deck, and park next to a large brown van that had a huge fake sign saying UPF. Once again, he would punch the hatch open. This time, the contents were transferred to the other vehicle, the hatch was closed, and they drove out of the deck. Norse watched in the rear-view mirror as two men in brown shirts and shorts took care of the transfer.

When they left the parking deck, Dominic would laugh and say, "Another week, another dollar," and they would then go on to have dinner somewhere. Norse got the impression that he was somehow very relieved that this job was done. In hindsight, it was obvious the relief was because of the amount of money that was being handled. And, it was, of course, all cash. The mob did not take checks or credit cards.

Harp decided that the target would be that UPF truck and began to plan where and when. The first step would be to see if the process continued in Dominic's absence. This time the rental was a small Nissan four-door sedan. They were waiting in a dark corner of that deck where they could see the ramp. It was a cool Saturday afternoon. They were positioned so that all traffic would have to go by them. They were the old couple again, she with the long gray hair, and he with the glasses and stupid hat. Norse studied Harp while they waited. He had leaned back and closed his eyes. She was concerned that he looked very tired.

They had about given up when the brown van came into the deck and proceeded up the ramp. Now they knew what was coming next. Sure enough, the black SUV with deeply tinted windows went by. In just over ten minutes, the black SUV came back down. They waited. The brown UPF truck exited next. The transfer had been made and, importantly, it was still on the same schedule, while the deck was relatively free of people. They followed the UPF van. It traveled at a leisurely pace through the city.

On the following Saturday, after the black SUV had gone down, a plain, used, Ford Explorer was stopped on the down ramp with yellow emergency sawhorses blocking its way. Both front doors were open. An elderly woman in obvious distress was lifting the shoulders and trying to pick up an old man who was lying on his back near the sawhorses. When she saw the brown van coming, she stopped trying to pick him up and ran to the van crying. She was waving her hands around helplessly, "They blocked the exit! My husband had a heart attack trying to move those things! I can't pick him up! What will we do? Help me!"

The two men in the van were very well trained and aware of the value of the load they carried. Both were well-armed. Yet, their options here were limited. They could easily push that car out of the way but they couldn't run over the old man with gray beard. If they thought they could get away with it, they would have simply shot both of them. After calling it in, and against all directives, they got out of the van with guns drawn, looking up and down the ramp. There was nothing threatening. The place was empty, and this was just a sick old man and his wife. They holstered the weapons and bent to pick up Harp.

Tasers are very easy to find. It is perfectly reasonable for an elderly woman afraid to walk the streets of Philly to buy two of maximum power. She wanted to be sure that the bad guy was put down and stayed down. Harp and Norse had firearms, his was under him on the pavement, hers was in her shoulder bag. They weren't needed. When the two men leaned over to pick up Harp, the one at his shoulders took the full charge under his chin. The man at his feet took the charge in the side of his neck. Watching Norse do her part, Harp was again impressed at her coolness in action. Both men lost all muscle control and dropped like stones.

Harp leaped to his feet and quickly put snap ties on their hands and feet. They opened a side door on the van and, with some difficulty, hoisted both bodies into the space behind the front seats. Norse grabbed the barriers and threw them in the back of the Ford. With Norse driving the Ford and Harp driving the van, they calmly drove from the parking deck. It all took less than two minutes. Their transfer point was a parking lot in a busy area near a popular restaurant. Nobody paid any attention to the people transferring packages from the ubiquitous UPF Van to an old Ford Explorer that had backed up to the van. Harp was tossing the bags from the van to the Ford where Norse was waiting. She would dump the contents into a very large suitcase then throw the empty bag back into the van. When they were done, they had a very large wheeled suitcase full of cash with some coins thrown in. Harp listened as communications with the van got more urgent. He watched as the van's operators slowly came around. When all the cash was in the suitcase, Harp hit both men with the taser again, took their wallets and firearms, locked all the van doors, and kept the keys. There was the remote but also several other keys on the ring. There was one more thing: In dayglow orange, Harp sprayed *NY calling!* on the side of the van.

As before, the rental was driven back to its place of business, the suitcase was put in Harp's big Ford SUV, and they drove back to Philadelphia. After wheeling the suitcase into the suite, Harp kicked off his shoes and collapsed on the sofa. "God, I am so tired," was all he said and started to fall asleep.

"No, Harp, get up. You need to go to bed." She began tugging on his arms. He groggily relented and allowed her to lead him like a child into his bedroom. She held him up while removing his shirt. He stood with eyes closed, half asleep already, while she loosened his belt and let his pants drop to the floor.

She gave him a gentle push and he fell backward into the bed wearing only his jockey shorts. She lifted his feet in and covered him after marveling at the scars that seemed to decorate his body from head to toe. He was out. Norse carefully checked the wounds to his head. The one on his forehead was still troublesome. It appeared to have a darker red swelling under the scar tissue that she didn't like. He seemed maybe a little feverish and slightly reddened.

Norse left to prepare for bedtime herself but came back to check on his condition while in her robe and pajamas. Now there was no doubt; his face was hot to the touch, and he was lifting his shoulders and twisting his hands as if reaching for something. Norse started bathing his face with cloths containing ice cubes while blaming herself for his condition. We tried too much too soon, she said to herself. He wouldn't have done all this if I hadn't been here. She continued until she, too, was very sleepy. Not really thinking what she was doing, she threw her robe over a chair and lay down next to Harp. On her side facing him, she gently stroked his face with her fingertips. He appeared to relax and fall into a deeper sleep. So did she.

Harp's eye's opened to a pleasant sight in the morning. He found Luna Norse sound asleep on her side facing him. She wore no makeup, her glasses were gone, and her hair had fallen to a point where it most attractively framed her face. Her mouth was slightly open and she was snoring with a soft purring sound. Her pajama top had twisted up and toward her side and one perfectly formed breast was displayed as if placed by an artist inches from his nose. He felt like crap. His head ached, his mouth was a military latrine, and he could smell his own body, but he was not about to make the slightest move to awaken her.

He didn't know why she was here or what she had done, but he was going to enjoy this moment as long as possible. The last thing he remembered was collapsing on the sofa with a desperate need to sleep.

She woke up to find Harp awake and watching her with a steady gaze and calm smile. Her first thought was pleasure that he seemed to be recovered from the fever. Then she remembered where she was. Then, she looked down and saw that something was uncovered. Her first instinct was to tug everything back into place. Luna then realized there was no threat here. She could trust him. She left the breast uncovered and met Harp's gaze. They reached an understanding in that gaze. She said, "I'm not ready yet."

Harp nodded. "I know. It's okay." She felt a sense of relief that they were still on the same page. She straightened her pajama top and got up somewhat reluctantly. It felt strangely normal to be lying there with this man.

He looked around and asked, "What happened?" Norse described the evening from the time they got back into the apartment.

"I guess I overdid it." Harp said. "I still feel kind of weak. Probably I should rest up for a couple of days."

Norse joked, "It will take us a couple of days just to count that money. I'll make breakfast and we'll get to it."

Harp's appetite had not suffered. He stuffed himself with eggs, sausage, and pancakes and watched while Norse, with some difficulty, dumped the contents of the suitcase onto the sofa. Piles of cash tumbled out and overflowed onto the floor. "Good God," she said in awe. It was a mixture of denominations but mostly twenties and hundreds. Some had been bundled and much of it was loose bills. Scattered among the bills were simple forms with handwriting.

Harp watched in amusement as Norse, still in her pajamas, poked and pulled from the pile as if it were a child's sandbox. She turned and whispered to Harp, "I have never seen this much money. I mean, in person. What the heck are we going to do with all this?"

"Not much, actually. We just took it as another poke at Donetti. We may need some cash for a couple of things, but the rest is yours to keep." Harp grinned. "You can take it back to Muncie—if we survive."

She turned to Harp, wide-eyed at the sudden confluence of two enormous thoughts: She could be rich and she could be dead. Norse shuddered and shook her head as if to shake the thought away. Before she started counting, she pulled the two pistols, the pieces of paper, and wallets from the pile and handed them to Harp. He was sipping coffee and watching Norse with amusement and affection. It was strange, he thought, how blasé she had become handling weapons—and now stolen wallets. It was strange, he thought, how comfortable he had become in her company. He had rarely spent this much time with one woman. And, he had definitely never spent this much time with a woman without at least trying to get her into the sack.

She finished counting. The total was $213,486.00. She sat staring at the now bundled bills stacked on the coffee table. "Do you know what, Harp? This must be the amount they have taken from people and businesses in just *one week!*"

Harp shrugged. "This has always been just part of doing business in this country and it always will be." He studied the forms they found among the bills. They were part of the mob's reporting system. It gave the names and amounts for the places that were paying for protection. Harp automatically looked for it, but The Battle was not on this list. There were other marks, a kind of code next to some of the addresses. He remembered seeing a list with these marks as he went through the wallets. It was a small, hand-written cheat sheet, probably not approved by the bosses. It provided the meaning of those marks. Going from the cheat sheet to the forms, Harp could guess from experience what most of the marks meant. On some of the lists, there were blanks where the amounts were written. An example in one case for this collection period was a place called Madolyn's Boutique that did not pay. The mark next to this business was just a "V." This could mean simply that it was time for a "visit." For another unpaid address there was a "W." This could mean "window." And for another, there was a "B" with an exclamation point. Harp was afraid that could mean either "burn" or "bomb." There were others for which he could not guess the meaning. And, he admitted to Norse, he was just guessing. They could just be accounting maneuvers, like cutting supplies or anonymous reporting to the state or federal governments on regulation violations. In the end, all the marks, the whole system of reports, were nothing but a series of directions for the mob's army of enforcers.

"But this is terrible," Norse cried after Harp explained what he thought was happening. "We know what they're doing to these poor people and we can't do anything about it!"

This gave Harp an idea. "There is something we can do. We can mail these lists with the cheat sheet to the police. It won't take them long to figure out what it all means. It won't change much, but it will provide a list of all the people Donetti is threatening. Maybe the cops can use it for something." Norse, wearing gloves again, made copies of everything using the copier in Kip's office and put the copies in a manila envelope for a later anonymous mailing. The originals, covered with their prints and perhaps other substances from which DNA could be withdrawn, were shredded and flushed.

Harp remained sitting at the kitchen table. He was still tired and his forehead was aching. Norse came back to the kitchen to find Harp with his head on his arms almost asleep. She was ashamed that she had completely forgotten to look at the swelling on his forehead. She found that it appeared to be slightly worse than the night before. Now she was really worried. Searching through all three bathrooms, she found an old, long expired, container of Amoxicillin. There were only eight pills. She then went to the internet to find instructions for making a poultice.

Back in the kitchen, she forced Harp to sit up and take two of the pills. With a simple poultice ready, she found that the best way to hold it to the wound and wrap the gauze tape around his head to hold it in place was to stand straddling his lap. Standing there in a casual intimacy often assumed when nursing the weak or infirm, she gave no thought to the ramifications of this position. When she was done wrapping the gauze, she was holding his head in both hands and looking into his striking gray eyes. These are the eyes of an animal, she thought, but now he is a sick animal. Harp just looked back at Luna Norse. Then he wrapped his arms around her and pulled her down against his chest. She did not resist. She sat, carefully cradling his wounded head in her arms, pulling it toward her chest. Neither knew exactly what they were thinking. It was simply a need to which both responded instinctively. They sat that way, enjoying each other's warmth.

Then she felt the pressure of something growing beneath her. Norse was startled at her own instinctive response to push back down against this sudden heat. Her body was ready–but her mind was not. She quickly pulled away and stood up. A disappointed Harp reluctantly let go. She smiled and pulled on his arms and said, "Come on, Harp. You need to get back into bed. Alone." Harp shook his head at his weakness but agreed. Again, he slept.

26

While Harp was sleeping, Norse was thinking. They had talked about the next thing they might do to madden Arturo, to bring him home. Harp knew that a confrontation was inevitable. He knew that they could not remain hidden forever. Plus, he realized that he just wanted his life back. He wanted to be in his condo and drink again at the Battle and get the new place up and going. And, there was only one way this could happen: Arturo Donetti must die. They could not go to Italy to do this, so Donetti must come back to Trenton.

They talked about the place where the Donetti mob enforcers met. The little Italian ristorante. Norse was trying to recall everything in minute detail about the time that Dominic had driven there to drop off the satchel full of cash. First she tried to find it on the web. It wasn't listed. If she had had access to a Trenton phonebook, she would find that it wasn't listed there either.

Norse decided that she now knew the way to Trenton from Philadelphia to drive it herself. So, while Harp was sleeping, she drove his big Ford Explorer to Trenton. Once there, she was lost. She didn't know that part of the city. Again, she relied on memory to finally recognize streets and locales through which Dominic had driven her. It took three hours, but she found herself on the street in front of the little place on the corner with only Pasta Calamarata over the door. It was closed and quiet. She now had an address. She thought she knew what Harp would need, so she took pictures from several different spots. She even drove down the street behind the place to capture that aspect.

Norse was not accustomed to doing one thing while at the same time watching everything happening in the area of the focus. Parked on the street, she was studying the photos on her phone when there was a knock on her window. Quickly palming the phone, she turned to the window to find an elderly man waiting. Norse cracked the window just enough to talk and hear. Consciously steadying her voice, she asked "Can I help you?"

"No, lady, I can help you. I can help you get the fuck out of my neighborhood." He lifted a cane and pointed down the street. "We don't like nosy people here taking pictures of our homes." He had watched as she drove from spot to spot taking pictures.

Norse nodded. "Okay. I was just thinking we might come to that cute little restaurant for dinner tonight." She added some stuffiness to her voice. "I didn't realize that this neighborhood was so unfriendly. You needn't worry. We won't be coming here. Ever." He said nothing more but stepped back and waved the cane as if giving directions. She took the hint and drove off. She easily drove directly to their apartment.

Harp was still asleep when she entered. Still keyed up from the trip to Trenton, she thawed some pork chops and prepared dinner to keep busy. She needed the distraction because she was worried about how Harp would respond to her trip to Trenton.

Harp awoke to the very pleasant aroma of pork frying and vegetables cooking. In the bathroom, he removed the poultice and looked again at all the rough edges of what used to be a fairly normal face. The swelling on his forehead was down some, but the scars from that wound were still very evident. While his growing hair was quickly covering the back and side wounds, the forehead scar was too visible and remained rough and angry. It also seemed to Harp that his left eye just didn't look the way it used to. His beard was steel gray and now two to three inches long. He thought of cutting it off, or at least trimming it, but decided that it was part of a disguise that he might still need. He settled for a long hot shower without the damned shower cap. The stitches were gone, the itching had stopped, and he had gotten used to the new rough spots in his scalp caused by the scar tissue. The hot water was a ritual cleansing. It was a huge step toward normalcy.

Harp's happy mood when he came from his room for dinner didn't last. Norse, after several false starts, blurted out, "You were sound asleep, so I drove to Trenton. We need to know where the Pasta Calamarata is if we're going to do something there." Harp scowled and started to speak but she held up a hand and continued. "I was careful not to do anything to attract attention. I found it! It's on a corner in an old neighborhood. We can look at it now on the Internet!"

In spite of himself, Harp was pleased at her initiative, though he was careful not to show it. While her trip was a success, there were too many things that could have gone wrong. He stood in front of her and put his hands on her shoulders. He held her gaze as he spoke. "What we are doing could get us both killed. The only way we survive is to always work as a team. I need to know at all times where you are and what you are doing so *no more surprises!*" Norse contrite, nodded. Harp continued, "Now, let's eat. I'm so hungry I could eat the ass out of a..." Harp remembered just in time that she would not appreciate that little bit of militaria and did not finish.

When finished eating, they went to Kip's office and looked up a map of Trenton. Knowing the address now, they quickly found the place that would be the focus of their next attack. The wonder of the Internet allowed them to zero in almost to the front door of the building. The difficulty of any frontal attack was soon obvious. The pasta store, which is how they referred to it, lay among many other small buildings on a narrow street in one of the older sections of the city. Norse related the conversation with the man who had confronted her. This meant that there was the possibility of an ad hoc system of lookouts in place. They could not see how they could conduct any operation against the place without jeopardizing innocent lives. Just leaving that neighborhood was a complicated maneuver that could easily put them in a position to be stopped by the police. Norse was expressing doubt that anything could be done at this location when Harp recalled something from his youth. He had grown up in Trenton and was pretty much free to roam the streets, he told Norse.

"No kid is going to be free to wander around the streets in a place like this," she objected.

Harp laughed grimly, "I was. From the age of ten, I was pretty much on my own. My father disappeared, and my mother drank herself to death. I was kicked around from place to place until I enlisted."

"That is so sad," she said.

"Yeah, well, life is hell for some people. Anyway, I remember collecting cans and bottles at a city park near there." He showed her where the park was on the map. "It was on a kind of ridge that looked down on that part of the city."

Norse looked where Harp had pointed. "So? That's blocks away from the store."

"Yes, but if there is a clear line of sight, I can make it work."

"You mean you can shoot someone from hundreds of feet away?" she asked incredulously.

"I can shoot someone from *thousands* of feet away." Harp said in a way that left no doubt that he had indeed done just that. Norse just shook her head in disbelief. "Anyway, I remember that park was in an artsy-fartsy neighborhood and was used by lots of artists because of the view. We need to get down there and see if the store is visible." He thought some more about the operation. "We can't hit the guy delivering the money. We can't blow the place up because of collateral damage. It looks like all we can do is shoot the place up. That should be enough to get Arty's attention. And, the best time to do this would be right after the delivery of the money. It should be close to dark when the streets will be mostly empty. Norse nodded. She was leaving the strategy up to the man who had done it all.

They drove another rental directly to the target. Harp studied the area as Norse drove. He could see immediately that there was no chance of a local attack. There just wasn't a safe place anywhere in the neighborhood to set up and then get away. With this conclusion, Harp decided to shift their attention to that park. He tried but could not see the park from any street near the target. It was looking pretty hopeless. They drove there nevertheless, just on the chance they could see the target. It seemed to Norse that it took forever to get to this small green oasis in the city. She could not imagine anyone actually hitting something from that far away.

Once at the park, they joined the many other people walking around or sitting on benches looking down at a part of the city that was basically nondescript but pleasant to observe from above. Humans were just another animal that enjoyed a view looking downward, perhaps because it provided an instinctive survival advantage through the eons. They were in their old folks disguises, she with long gray hair, maroon blouse, and long pleated hippy skirt; he with baggy khakis, cheap shirt, glasses, gray beard, and stupid hat. They were holding hands and appeared to be softly conversing as they would stroll and stop, looking downward, trying to spot this tiny place among all the buildings below. She was saying that she did not see a thing. He was intently studying the arrangement of streets. As they walked, different buildings would come into view through the trees of the park and then vanish behind other buildings. Then, Harp suddenly squeezed her hand and stopped. "There it is."

Norse turned to look in the direction of his gaze and said with some anxiousness, "I don't see it, Harp."

Harp was now locked on. While holding her hand and just murmuring, he proceeded to take her eyes down the streets and across the blocks that would lead her to the target. With his help, she finally found it. She was dismayed. She turned to Harp, "Harp, that is just a little spot between all these buildings. We can't do anything from here!"

Harp smiled. There was no way he could ever explain all the training, the instincts, the nuances, the mental preparedness that he could bring to bear when needed. So, instead, he smiled and replied, "No, Luna, this is ideal." Harp took out a phone; it was just another burner, but the people around them wouldn't know that, and pretended to take pictures. But, he was backing up as he held the phone up to his eyes. He now had a target, and a plan was coming into shape. He continued backing away until he was in the parking area next to the park. Norse followed in puzzlement. The spot was found. Harp stood in a parking spot where an open door of a van could have a view of the target. He calculated that it was about 500 yards. Easy. "Luna, look around. It's going to happen next Sunday. Study this spot. Commit it to that memory of yours. You are going to drive to this spot and park so an open minivan door is *exactly* where I am standing. Two feet either way and it won't work."

"What am I going to be doing?" Harp appreciated that she was all in. She did not question what he was planning to do. She could be a real warrior, he thought.

"You are going to drive to this spot in a plain older minivan. We will be the old folks out for a Sunday drive getting here. You will drive very carefully because there will be a weapon in the back. When we are close, I am going to get into the back and sit on the floor facing the van door on the driver's side. I will be covered with a dark cloth of some sort." Norse was nodding and absorbing all of this. Harp continued, "You will then open the van door and carefully follow my instructions on placement of the van. The interior lights will be disabled. After I have acquired the target, you will look in all directions and give me the all clear or stand down. I can wait. There should be minimal traffic. What I am going to do should take no more than twenty to thirty seconds. It won't be loud, but it could be heard, so I will be quick."

"Suppose this spot is taken?"

"Then we will wait until this spot is clear. As long as the lights are on inside the target, I can do it." Harp was going to use the silenced rifle and scope that they had taken from the mob's gun shop. It wasn't a night scope, so he needed the light in the target to be on. He had two twenty round clips and he was going to empty both. He knew this rifle was good at distances even greater than this but that the silencer would cut that to some degree. He figured that the first shot would tell the story and those that followed could be adjusted accordingly.

Harp finished the instructions. "The last thing you are going to do will be right after I have emptied the second clip. You are going to close the van door and dial 911 on one of our burner phones. You are going to scream in panic that there is a terrible gunfight going on at the target's address, with bullets flying everywhere. Plead for help, then hang up. I'll take the battery and card out of the phone and we'll hit the road back to Philly." He went on. "I'm guessing that several cops will converge on this place before all the guys in the back can get away. And, I'm guessing that the law would just love to get their hands on these guys."

As they were on the road back to Philly, Harp asked Norse, "Luna, I want you to think real hard about this. Did either one of us ever touch with our bare hands any of the stuff we took from that place behind the tile shop?"

Norse took her time. "Let's see, we went in with gloves and put everything in that duffle bag with gloves. We brought that bag back to the apartment and put it in your closet. We might have touched the bag, but I don't think we have touched anything in it since. Why?"

"Think about this. I am going to use a rifle we took from that place. At the very least, the guy who did the work there touched it. Plus, it could still have the prints of the man who brought it in. And, we are going to use cartridges that could very likely have other prints on them." Harp was thinking as he talked. "Suppose that, after we use it on the target, this rifle and spent cartridges end up in the hands of the cops?" Harp laughed, "I would bet my ass that whatever prints they found on these things would be on record and that they would belong to one of the guys in Donetti's mob."

Norse shook her head in wonder. "That's diabolical–and wonderful. It would drive everybody nuts trying to figure out who did what." She thought some more. "That could mean to them that someone from the inside did the dirty deed."

Harp leaned back against the headrest, "Then that's just what we're going to do."

27

It went as planned. They had to wait until the parking spot was adequately distanced from people and autos. Norse drove in and opened the van door with the driver's control button.

"Another foot forward," Harp directed. He was sitting knees up with his back against the opposite sliding door. She carefully inched forward.

"Okay, stop. I've got it."

"All right. I'm getting out," she said. Norse exited the van and strolled a ways looking at her cell phone as everyone now seemed to do. She was actually studying the area. It was dark and empty. Norse casually walked back to stand beside the open van door, still looking at her phone. Quietly, she said, "It's all clear. Go ahead." She set herself. She was wearing ear plugs. Her job was to now stand next to the van door looking at her phone and act as if she did not hear a thing as the rifle was fired. Harp had explained in detail how she was totally free from any danger, but her presence behaving in an unconcerned manner would allay any immediate attachment of the noise to the van. She thought she was ready.

The mob had somehow gotten its hands on a military

M-110 SASS (semi-automatic sniper system) rifle, a version of the M-14, and added the silencer. It was different from the usual weapon used for sniping in that it was not bolt action. It shot the standard .308 cartridge, which has tremendous range and hitting power in semi-auto mode. It was not made in fully automatic mode. This was the rifle they had taken from the elicit gunsmith's shop. Like all military rifles, it would take several different-sized clips. The clips taken from the shop held twenty rounds, so that was what Harp used. Any fingerprints on the weapon and cartridges were still those that were on it when they took them. Harp was also very careful not to leave even the slightest particle of his DNA. He was fully aware of the strides forensics had made in identifying miscreants. One hair or flake of skin in the wrong place was enough to convict a person—even in the absence of any other corroborative evidence.

The first shot was high, so Harp adjusted. It was an excellent scope. He emptied the first clip in four seconds and the second clip a little more slowly. He had gotten the range and was now shooting at more specifics in the store. The bartender was quickly on the floor behind the bar and out of the action. All the windows and the back-bar bottles and mirror were already shattered into pieces. Harp then focused on the door to the rear room and a narrow strip of wall next to the door. All he could see from this elevation was the bottom third of each, so he sent several rounds through those. The bullets easily penetrated both, going into the room beyond. What they did there he could not know. He finished the second clip in 10 seconds. The store absorbed 40 rounds in the space of about 20 seconds in all. All the empties were on the floor of the van.

He was done "Luna!" He had to shout it twice before she responded. "Luna! Get in! Close the door!"

She moved as if in a trance but climbed into the front seat and closed both doors. "Luna, you've got to get us out of here." He reached over the seat and roughly shook her shoulder. "Come on, move!"

She finally started the engine and drove away. She was muttering, "Jesus, Jesus, Jesus."

Harp shook her again, "Make the call! Hurry!"

Norse shuddered and seemed to visibly recover from a trauma. Harp dialed 911 and handed her a phone and said, "Go!"

The panic in Norse's voice was made much more real by the experience of standing very close to the blast of forty rounds from a high-powered rifle. Even though it was supposedly silenced, it was still bright and concussive. Her voice accurately conveyed the sense of near panic she was feeling. She screamed in a ragged, tearful voice, "You got to get down here. There's a godawful gunfight going on! People are getting shot! The whole place is shot up! Help us! Please! It's that pasta place on the corner of Dillman and Prother! Oh, my god! Get down here!" Then, in response to the dispatcher, "Yes, the corner of Dillman and Prother! Hurry! They're shooting right now!" She hit the off button and handed the phone to Harp who removed the battery and card. Harp urged Norse to hurry. They needed to be far away when the police shut down that part of the city. They could hear the sirens coming in from all directions as they hit the Interstate going north.

Within an hour, Harp and Norse were back in the condo. During the drive, Harp was busy. The rifle was broken down and packaged in plastic bags in a peculiar way with just the tip of the barrel showing. Both were exhausted. It was late. Each stumbled off to their respective bedrooms. Harp managed to shed his clothes and fall into his bed. He was asleep in seconds. He slept so soundly, he was not aware that Norse had crept in with her own blanket and had carefully lain on the bed beside him. In spite of her determination to support Harp in this campaign against Donetti and in spite of her own desire for retribution, the magnitude of what they were doing had finally gotten to her. She was frightened, unsure, and emotionally tired. But, as she lay there looking at the soundly sleeping Harp, she was somewhat reassured by his confidence in his abilities. In his blissfully ignorant presence, she finally slept.

28

No one was sleeping anywhere near the corner of Dillman and Prother. After the first unit arrived and described the magnitude of the situation, it became a priority response for all units in the area and for gearing up a SWAT team. Within ten minutes the entire area was secured. Blue lights, red lights, and reflections of both lights in all the windows of the neighborhood were lighting up the sky. The men in the back room were not amateurs. They had an escape plan. The three who weren't wounded quickly exited through a side door into the neighboring building. They went through that building to an exit into the alley behind the stores and began to run north to get to cars that had been called and that were supposed to be waiting. The cars weren't waiting, but the police were. The mob hit men found themselves confronted by several police with guns drawn leaning over the hoods of their cars. Their job was to stop anyone coming out of this alley. Their choice was clear. Give up or die. Two gave up. One died of multiple gunshot wounds.

Two of the men in the back room could not run. One just inside the wall next to the door had been hit in the hip and was painfully immobilized. The other had been hit in the leg by a bullet that had ricocheted off the floor. He could move but was busy trying not to bleed to death.

When the site of the action had been secured, the police began to take stock of what had happened. By now an assistant chief was present. He whistled in awe as he studied the damage done by Harp's bullets. These lethal projectiles had just about blown everything up. All the front windows were gone. Even the wooden bar was splintered. There was glass everywhere crunching under their feet. The back room was also heavily marked by the bullets that came through just a small area in the door and wall. There was blood and splinters and money scattered everywhere. The assistant chief got an urgent call while he was still in that room, looking back out toward the front, trying to get a handle on what had happened. The call informed him that the men they now had in custody were four well-known mob enforcers who worked for the Donetti mob. Two were wounded in the attack. One was dead, shot by police while trying to escape. They could hold two on old warrants but had nothing on the other two. They did what they could, however, and published photos of all of them to law enforcement agencies nationwide. These photos were somehow leaked to the public with the admonition in the sensation rags that they were extremely dangerous and would kill anybody anytime they felt like it. This basically ruined their effectiveness as mob enforcers. They planned to move to new territories.

The precinct's detective experts were already at work. They quickly found that the bullets were the common .308 round, maybe military. It was determined that the shots came from an elevation above and to the right of the store. They first thought that this would be the roof of one of the buildings down one of the streets. This possibility was eliminated in the light of the morning when it became obvious that no one could have gotten up on any roof that had the necessary sight angle. This assumption wasted a lot of time. They were stymied until a rifle-carrying guard standing in front of the store had the bright idea of looking sharply upward off in the distance through a rifle scope. When he did that, he found himself looking up at the trees along the horizon. Those trees lined a street in a small park about a quarter mile away. Several cars raced to that location. Looking back down at the store, he had no doubt that this was the location of the shooter. A canvas of the area found only one person who remembered hearing strange tapping sounds like a hammer hitting wood a long way off. He assumed it was someone building or repairing something. As for suspect vehicles, there was nothing. Cars came and went at all hours and nobody paid them any attention. How could someone, the shooter, fire off forty-some rounds of a high-powered rifle and nobody notice a damned thing? Adding to the consternation was the simple message spray painted on the sidewalk: *NY Calling.* They didn't know whether or not this was related to the shooting. They took photos for the record.

The big question in everyone's mind was *why?* Who was doing this? Was it a gang war? What weapon was used? It didn't take long for the law to figure out that the little restaurant was the regular meeting place for this bunch of killers. So, if it was a Donetti hangout, who would want to hit it so hard? Then, to confuse things, a patrolman in Trenton was returning to his car from a doughnut stop and nearly tripped over a long bundle lying on the ground beside the driver side door. He was about to kick it out of the way when he noticed one thing that is perhaps not the most common but is universally recognized, the end of a gun barrel. He first froze, then had the sense to call it in. The package was about 34 inches long. It was carefully opened to find an M-14 sniper rifle in pieces, carefully wrapped. There was a printed note which read simply: *Used at Dillman and Prother.* The rifle was covered in finger prints. A quick run of the prints showed they belonged to one of the mobsters who was in the building at the time of the attack! Harp had been very careful not to leave a single fingerprint or DNA marker on the weapon they had taken from the gunsmith's shop. A coordinated effort was undertaken to investigate how this could happen—and who the hell was doing this.

Someone far away was agonizing over the same questions. Arturo Donetti, still in Italy, was in a stomping, screaming rage. He had just lost his cadre of enforcers; one dead, two wounded, and two being watched around the clock. He would now be seen as weak and not in control. He made up his mind. He had to go home. He had to put this thing with that shit Harper on the back burner until he figured this thing out. He planned to arrive back in Trenton and take over everything personally. He would be there within two days.

As a matter of fact, everybody was eagerly waiting for his arrival. The local police, the state police, and the New Jersey Bureau of Investigation. Also, unknown to all of these enforcement agencies, there was another group of people who were waiting. It was the loose confederation of New York City mobs who were getting very irritated at the questions that had arisen of late.

First it was reps from the Donetti mob asking what was going on. Why were they doing all this shit in the Trenton area? Now, the latest contacts to New York were guys from the NJBI wondering why they hit a little store in Trenton with such dev-astating effect. The response to all of them was: We don't know what the fuck you're talking about. We ain't done anything. We ain't gonna do anything, but if you keep buggin' us, we might have to do something. After several such inquiries, it was deter-mined that a New York guy needed to go down to Trenton and have a little chat with this fuckin' Arty Boots.

29

Harp and Norse had carried out an exhaustive study on the next target. Harp had been fascinated by the claim that the Donettis had a "ton" of money, and it was held at this private and very secret location that was apparently also one of their residences. Norse had spent hours trying to recreate the route she and Dominic had taken to get there. It was made more difficult because they had only gone there once and because of the horrendous things that had happened to her there. Rather than trying to forget the place completely, she was now trying to remember every detail of the visit. She remembered a long drive in the woods of New Jersey north of Trenton. Unfortunately, it was a road without many markers, even for her prodigious memory. It was finally pinned down when Norse recalled looking out the window of their bedroom and seeing a forestry lookout tower in the distance.

With this major clue, they were able to calculate pretty much exactly where she must have been standing. They then went to government information sites and, after looking at aerial maps, they spotted it. It was just a dot on a satellite map but, by zooming in, they found a property almost totally obscured by trees.

Another key point in her memory was that Norse remembered looking down into a fairly steep ravine from their bedroom window. This provided the information Harp needed on the type of topography. The conclusion was that the money was being held in a two-story home with a basement, on the edge of a ravine, a long way from any neighbors, about twenty miles northwest of Trenton. It had electrically-operated gates, paved drive, a large parking area in front of the house, and was probably wired and well-guarded. Whether or not the money was there, this was still one of the places that the Donettis stayed, even if only temporarily. Harp suspected that the remoteness and implied secrecy of the property gave it greater likelihood of hiding something significant.

The first thing they had to do was get a look at the place. This would take Harp on a hike through the woods. To prepare for that, Harp and Norse paid a 2 a.m. visit to the other bar that he had bought those many weeks ago. Harp knew Tommy was making sure that the building was well tended even though it had been closed all this time. The apartment upstairs had the kind of equipment Harp needed for this next move against Donetti. It had all belonged to the former owners, Edgar and Hal Priest. Edgar said that his brother's hunting gear was stored in the back room. Harp looked at it briefly before and remembered camo clothing, boots, shotguns, hats, packs, etc.

Norse was now very familiar with the drive from Philadelphia. With Harp's directions, she drove directly to Ed and Hal's bar where Harp let himself in at the side door. Using a very small flashlight, he moved quickly to the storage room. Because it was windowless, he closed the door and turned on the overhead lights. Now that he was carefully examining everything in the room, he was amazed at the number of things available to outdoor sportsmen. In addition to the usual stuff were scents, paints, warmers, coolers, special underwear, hydrators, goggles, and more. Harp packed what he needed into another large duffle and returned to the truck. They drove back to Philly and went to their separate beds. He was really tired again and his head still hurt a little.

Two mornings later, Norse drove Harp to the road that led to the Forestry Department tower. As expected, it was chained, so he began his hike at the entrance to the road. He was dressed in all camo and carrying enough food for one day and night. He had hand and foot warmers, fur-lined hat, and water for one day and night. He was equipped with a compass, hunting knife, binoculars, and a silenced 9 mm that they had stolen from the gunsmith shop. He also carried a game camera—which was to be the reason for being out there. He was just looking at sites to set up a camera watching for wildlife. They had calculated that he would have to hike about two miles cross country to get to the house. He was then going to find a spot where he could observe activity around the place to be sure it was a Donetti property. He did not want to carry out his plan if this was home to someone else.

Harp was in place at daylight, leaning back against a large tree on the top of the slope on the other side of the ravine. This spot provided a good view of the house and courtyard. With the camo clothes, face paint, and pieces of brush he had pulled up over his legs, he was invisible to anyone in the house. He spent the morning relaxing and watching. It was pretty easy to discern the room where Norse stayed. There were only a couple of windows on the ground floor that would have given a clear view of the tower. He spotted no guards or lookouts. He could not see any wires, cameras, or traps around the place. It looked like their assumption was that the steepness of the ravine and isolation of the property made it safe from incursion from his direction. At exactly 11:30 a.m., a black sedan pulled into the courtyard in front of the main entrance. A man came from the house and met another man wearing a sling for his right arm who was slowly getting out of the car. Harp thought that they both looked familiar. He was surprised, then furious, when he realized what he was seeing. The man coming from the house was Booge and the man known as Frat Boy exiting the car was the guy who had tried to kill him. How had this son of a bitch gotten out of custody?

It didn't matter now. This was without a doubt a Donetti property. The plan was on.

Harp studied the house with new intensity. He knew which room Norse was in. If what Dominic said was true, the ton of money was in the room underneath that sat on a foundation wall several feet high. This side of the house extended several feet further down because of the slope. So, Harp eyeball-measured where another room would be under those windows and then studied the point where the bottom of that floor would meet the rock of the slope. When that point was determined, he carefully planned his route to get to it, and get away from it. He called Norse for a pickup. He wouldn't have to stay any longer.

They were back in the late afternoon of the next day. This time the back pack was put to an entirely different use, carrying a special package. Harp walked the same route and came to the observation post he had earlier established. After watching for any activity and seeing none, he proceeded. Moving slowly and carefully, trying to make as little noise as possible, he came to the spot at the base of the structure he had already selected. With comfortable ease, he pulled a tightly wrapped square object from the back pack. Digging just enough to get the object tightly wedged between the wall of the house and the bedrock of the ravine wall, he roughly pushed it into place. After again studying its location and the foundation of the house, he shrugged and moved across the ravine and took shelter behind a large tree. First, he took a silenced nine-millimeter from a holster under his arm, then took out a cell phone and, without hesitation, dialed a number.

Harp had much experience with explosives. He had thrown and shot grenades. He had fired every kind of explosive ammunition. He had blown up ammo dumps and detonated huge IEDs. So, he was familiar with the stuff they had taken from the gunsmith's shop. It was Pentaerythritol Tetranitrate, or PETN, otherwise known as Semtex. It was a very stable explosive that required considerable shock to set it off–but Harp knew how to do it. What Harp didn't know was how much to use in this circumstance. He did not know how thick that foundation wall was, for instance. With all his experience in blowing things up, he had never blown up a modern American house. So, in true Harp warrior fashion, he said fuck it and used it all. In a way, he was wrong. Half of it would have been plenty.

But, then again, Arturo Donetti was wrong, too. He thought you could take a basement room with ordinary poured concrete floor and cinderblock walls and safely add many thousands of pounds of half-inch-thick quality steel to the walls, plus a thick steel door, and do this on top of the ordinary foundation on which the house had originally been built. He wanted a vault for his secret hoard of cash, and he wanted it strong enough to withstand any kind of robbery attempt. It was very well done. It was a fifteen by fifteen by nine room. It held large tubs of cash in the process of being counted and steel shelves all around, all with stacks of bills, supposedly a ton of them. It was environmentally controlled so that the temperature and moisture levels were perfect for storing cash.

Harp dialed the number, opened his mouth, and covered his ears. Even with his incredible experience, he was not prepared for the blast. Even the two-foot thick tree he was hiding behind flexed enough for him to feel it on his back. He waited with head covered until debris quit falling before he turned and looked at what he had wrought. The foundation and first floor on this end of the house was gone. He had misjudged where the side of the vault/room would be. He also misjudged the force that would be directed outward from the unyielding bedrock. Instead, Harp blew out the whole foundation on this end of the building, and most of it had fallen off to become a pile of rubble. He saw carpets, furniture, fixtures, and wood shards jumbled together on the side of the slope. Then, an even more bizarre sight awaited. Further down, at the bottom of the ravine, he saw what looked like a separate room itself lying almost intact. Those carefully welded metal walls had created a solid structure that held together even as it separated from the house. He almost burst out laughing. He had never seen anything quite so completely unexpected and ridiculous.

While still crouched cautiously beside the tree, getting ready to move, he saw Booge and Frat Boy run from the front of the house and start down the slope to see what had happened. They moved to their right and were looking up at the damage in awe.

Then, they realized that the person who had done this might still be here. Both wheeled around to crouch with guns ready, looking in all directions. When they looked up at his position, Harp fired. Booge fell limply backward against the slope. Frat Boy took three rounds before he fell across Booge's legs. Just as a precaution, Harp moved to collect the spent shells. He found three but could not spend any more time looking.

Seeing no further movement, Harp hurried down to the vault. Even strong as it was, one corner had split open from the impact when it had hit solid stone on the way to the bottom. Money was falling out of a three-foot wide gap into the active little stream there. The size of this blast, even in this isolated location, would probably get attention from someone, so he knew he would have to move fast. Though not quite up to speed, he thought he should be able to carry a backpack full of bills. He didn't care how much it was. What mattered was the shock to the Donetti mob. From long experience he knew that the backpack weighed more than 100 pounds after he had totally filled it. He was about to swing it up on his back when he noticed again that the money was dropping out of the vault and drifting downstream. With a grin, he reached in and pulled a bunch more, maybe a couple million, into the water. He then loaded up and began the hike out. When he got to the car, Norse was waiting but was very anxious. As soon as she saw him, she started gesturing for him to hurry. Harp covered the last fifty yards totally spent. She opened the rear door, and he threw the backpack onto the floor and started stripping. He threw all the camo gear onto the floor over the backpack. When he was down to the khakis and button-down shirt and with the stupid hat on, he ran around and got in the front seat.

When they were on a busy highway, she finally asked, "What in God's name did you do? I swear that explosion rocked the car!"

Harp was sitting with his head back against the rest, still trying to catch his breath, smiled. "I maybe used a little more than I needed."

Norse was still chagrined. "Well, everybody within five miles, maybe ten miles, must have heard that."

"Yeah, that's why I hurried." He added, "I was really, really glad to see you waiting, Luna. I don't think I could have gone another hundred feet."

She was mollified. "Tell me what happened. All of it."

30

Harp tiredly related everything that had happened. He left out the part about killing Booge and Frat Boy. She drove while listening, dumbfounded at the audacity of his actions. When he told her about the entire room tumbling down the slope, he laughed and then she laughed. He told her about the corner splitting and the money pouring into the small stream. He wondered aloud where it would end up–who would get it and what would they do with it.

"How much did you take, then?" she asked.

"Damned if I know. I guess it's around a hundred pounds of hundreds, however much that is."

"What are we going to do with that, Harp? You can't just pay cash for everything anymore."

"Let's worry about that later. As far as I'm concerned, you can have it all. We'll work that out later. Right now, I need a nap."

He was worried that he had gone too far for Norse, but all she said was, "A hundred pounds?"

Harp fell asleep to the gentle rocking of the car, leaving Norse driving and wondering what the hell had happened since she met this man.

What Harp did not and could not relate was what happened at the Donetti estate after he trudged away through the woods. For instance, he didn't see the second floor over the empty space left by the falling vault, now with no support, collapse into a pile of planks, furniture, carpets, and fixtures. The entire mass slid down the bank of the ravine, pushing a mound of soil and rock, which covered the bodies of Booge and Frat Boy. He didn't see the two thick cable ends that were torn loose and left exposed. They were the heavy kind that were driving the air conditioning for the vault. The pile of debris pushed one bare cable end just enough to touch another one. There was a violent yellow white arc, and they were blown apart only to be pushed back together again. This time they welded. Both cables quickly turned white hot, eagerly conveying a path of fire through the flammable materials in the rubble pile. Combustion of these materials once holding the house together was slow to start but quickly progressed upward until that whole side of the house was burning.

There was a couple charged with maintaining the property, ignoring what they heard and witnessed and keeping their mouths shut. Yvgeny and Polina Sigorvitch were Russians with green cards they had received through connections with the mob. They had been eating dinner in their garage apartment when the blast came. Even though it rocked the garage and spilled their borscht, they looked at each other and silently agreed to ignore it. That's what they were paid for. But then, the silence got to Yvgeny. When he stepped from their apartment, he saw the reflection of flames on the trees across the ravine. There were no fire alarms. The last thing the Donettis wanted was the police and fire departments to race to this veritable hideout. Yvgeny ran past the courtyard to the edge of the ravine. He saw too much for his mind to absorb all at once. The whole ravine side of the house was on fire, that end of the house had fallen off, and one large box-like section of the house was lying in the ravine. He knew his job here was over. Yvgeny had seen the steel door to Mr. Donetti's special room. He knew what he was looking at even though his mind told him it was impossible that it would be lying way down there atop the little brook. Tentatively approaching what he knew to be Mr. Donetti's vault, he could see, even in the dancing red light from the fire, the cash that was still tumbling from the opening. He removed his shirt and started filling it with bundles of cash, perhaps fifteen or twenty pounds in all. Thus laden, he ran back to the apartment and ordered a frightened Polina to quickly pack as much as she could. They had to leave as soon as possible. A fire like this would not go unnoticed.

Within a half hour, Yvgeny and Polina were speeding toward the gate. They had the remote for the gate in their car. They left it open. Once clear of the property, Yvgeny called a number. When it was answered, he related what was happening. Then he took the battery from the phone and they disappeared. He had lots of money now and cousins in Orlando.

The fire grew in the darkness to the point where it was evident from a long way off. It was assumed first that it was a forest fire. The New Jersey Forestry fire suppression units raced to the site. The location of the property was on the records of the state and local governments, so the large forest fire control units were quickly on their way. When they arrived at the house and saw the true nature of the fire, they immediately called the local fire department, which sent several units with large tanks. By this time, the house was fully involved. The forestry units focused on preventing the flames from reaching surrounding trees and brush. The fire department basically continued spraying the burning pile the house had become. As the structure burned, parts continually fell down the slope. It was assumed that the piece of the house already down there was a result of the fire. Soon, the bodies of Booge and Frat Boy were buried under a combination of ash, wood pieces, and mud.

While looking for possible sources of water to fill the tanks of the fire trucks, a fireman clambered down to the stream. With his ultra-bright flashlight, he was assessing the depth of the water when he saw hundred-dollar bills floating by. Picking up several with mouth open in wonder, he trudged upstream to find the source. Then he shined the light into the gap in the structure. He saw a mixture of fallen shelving, plastic tubs, and pallets, all covered with, or on top of, bundled cash money. "Holy Mother of God!" he said, as he picked up more money. He had his com radio and called the captain covering the fire to get his ass down here as goddamned fast as possible. The captain took one look and got on his radio. This was out of any local jurisdiction, so he called the state police. They were on their way anyway, so they arrived quickly. The trooper on call took one look and called his commander. Before he hit the road, the commander called the FBI, just in case it was in their purview. The FBI, after seeing the inside of the vault, alerted the IRS just to keep all the players up to date.

On the second day, the fire was totally extinguished. The fire inspectors and insurance people were going over the wreckage to determine the cause. The focus was soon on that room that had somehow fallen away from the house. It was soon determined that it had not fallen away. It had been *blasted* away. Now it was a criminal investigation. Now the ATF was called. The Bureau of Alcohol, Tobacco and Firearms covered explosions. A large bulldozer was brought in just to push the vault away from the stream and bring it to a level position. The lock for the vault door was soon cut away and the door opened. It was with incredible wonder that all the witnesses viewed the contents. Even jaded IRS agents had never seen anything like this. Most of the "ton" of money was still there. A few hundred pounds were gone, but no one would even know how much because the amount of money in this vault was known only to one man. He was neither present nor talking. Unfortunately, he had recently decided to store a few ounces of heroin in with the money, strictly for private use. Because there was a stash of drugs in with the money, it was all legally seized by the Federal Government. Thus, Mr. Arturo Donetti had lost ownership of about 96 million dollars due to the actions of Sergeant Horace B. Harper. In the process of leveling the vault room, the bulldozer pushed a thick layer of rock and dirt over the bodies of Booge and Frat Boy and compacted it to create a cheerful little level area next to the stream. A very pretty gazebo would one day be built on that spot.

31

The explosion at Arturo Donetti's secluded country estate initiated several separate actions. The first had begun at the same time as the serious morning investigations into the explosion and fire. Harp and Norse had awakened still tired but vindicated. They had each gone to their separate beds, leaving the new mass of cash on the floor in the kitchen where Harp dropped it. With coffee made, Norse was anxious to count it. To Harp, the amount was almost irrelevant. He had no use for it. He really didn't think of it as his. So, he shrugged and helped an excited Norse count. It turned out that Harp had carried away 107 pounds of 100-dollar bills. They weighed it on the bathroom scales just to see how close he had guessed it before it was unpacked and stacked.

He was shocked to learn that he had somehow walked away with about 4.85 million dollars and change. Now, for the first time, he was worried about the path he had chosen. This was too much. He had wanted to strike back–to hurt Donetti–to make him pay–but he didn't want the burden that comes with too big a prize. He remained thoughtful while Norse was excitedly moving stacks of money around the table. He understood the limitations of cash. It is very difficult to spend large amounts of it. You have to have a reason to own cash. Worse, you can't spend large amounts without explaining how you got it. What the hell was he going to do with this shit?

* * *

For the record, the property Harp had destroyed was owned by a corporation registered in Belize. It merely confirmed that the person using the property was a well-known mobster, Arturo "Arty Boots" Donetti. Mr. Donetti's location was unknown. He was thought to be in Italy. But, new communications with law enforcement in Italy showed that he had very recently left the country by private conveyance. His destination was unknown. That's all authorities in both countries knew. In the ashes, the investigators found a nearly intact set of ancient dueling pistols. It had been sitting on a mantel in an upstairs bedroom and was among the last things to fall into the wreck of the fire-engorged building below. The outside of the old walnut case was badly burned, but the pistols and little brass plaque inside were relatively untouched. It read: *To: Arturo Bignelli Donetti for: Taking Care of The Gando Thing.* It was further proof that this was indeed the property of the mobster known as Arty Boots. This sent the investigations off in a new direction. The authorities now knew for certain whose money they had seized and whose house had burned. They also knew the owner of that stash of drugs found in the vault. They had enough to bring him in. The word went out. Find Arturo Donetti. He was now a wanted man. Further, research also began on "The Gando Thing." Maybe there was something else they could hang on Arty's head.

* * *

Another Federal agency became very interested in the affairs of Arty Boots. Records showed there were extremely inadequate taxes paid on the money in the vault. A quick look at his payment history showed that Donetti had been claiming a modest income along with considerable business expenses. Efforts began by the Internal Revenue Service to secure a significant portion of the seized fortune as money owed to the government. Arty became a very important target of the IRS. The word went out. Find him.

* * *

In all these efforts to find Arty, all former connections were visited. These included hundreds of former low-level enforcers, collectors, counters, etc. They uniformly ducked their heads and tried to remain out of sight. One former contact, however, welcomed the questions. It was his former wife and mother of Dominic, Arva Winestone Donetti. She despised Arty. She learned to hate everything about him. Arva had harbored no illusions during her marriage to Arty. She knew what he was and what he did. She thought, however, that she could live apart from his mob life. Mostly, it worked. She had lived with their only son Dominic, enjoying the lush life in a beautiful estate with the best of everything readily available. But things Arty did would filter down. She learned to close her ears to stories of shootings, theft, and unbelievably cruel actions. She tried to reason with Arty. She questioned his need to do these things. We're rich, she would say, why can't we just travel and live the easy life?

Why do you have to live this way? Arty would shrug and say she didn't understand. It was all just business. And, besides, he could not walk away. He was in too deep. He knew too much.

Their relationship deteriorated to the point where they rarely communicated. The final nail in the coffin in which their marriage lay, ready to inter, was initiation of Dominic into the mob life. He was a good kid who had a chance to go straight. He was into sports at the exclusive Winston Academy, where he attended school from K through twelve. He got decent grades and had been accepted at Wharton School of Business due to huge donations she had made with Arty's money to the school's building fund. Arva had been a good mother. She believed that her Little Dommy was on his way into the world of legitimate business. Then, when Dominic was twenty-one, a sophomore at Wharton, Arty offered him a part-time job in what Arty called "Asset Management." This turned out to be nothing but moving cash from place to place. Dominic thought the work was fun. He decided to do it full time and to not go back for his junior year in college. Why go back, he reasoned, when he was already making more money than he would as a college graduate. He thus secured his father's blessing and broke his mother's heart. The divorce came about soon after. She was given all that she asked for and became a very rich and angry divorcee. When Dominic was killed during the conduct of his work for Arty, her heart was broken again. Her hatred of Arty was a wound that would not heal. She would do anything she could to get back at him.

When told of what happened to Arty's country estate, Arva laughed and clapped her hands in joy. The only thing that would have made her happier would be to learn of his death. She was happy to tell the authorities everything she knew. She told them of other secret residences. She told them where he stayed when in Italy. She related what she knew of secret foreign accounts. She tried to connect him to some of the atrocities she knew of. When she was finished, Arty was as good as dead. He was wanted on so many counts, any arrest would result in a lifetime behind bars. And that was just the authorities. That did not take into account all the former associates who expected payment for services rendered, regardless of the events in Arty's life. They were sorry for Arty's loss, sure, but business was business.

* * *

Eight days after the fire, a brown work van drove up the long drive to the Donetti house and stopped in the courtyard. A man in coveralls and work shirt got out with a clipboard and began a walking tour of the wreckage. He was wearing sunglasses and a ball cap. He appeared to be taking photos from time to time and making notes. He was especially interested in the ravine side of the mess, giving long study to the vault, now lying empty, in the ravine. He was still attempting to absorb the loss of all that money. How could ninety some million bucks just be taken away? He studied the open door to his prized vault and shook his head.

His story, if asked, was that he was developing an estimate on the costs of site clean-up. The reality was that this was Arturo Donetti who simply had to see this treasured property, which was now a symbol of the wreckage that was his life. He just wanted the answer to one simple question, and that was: who had done this? Who had hit their secret gun shop, the collection van, the pasta store, and now this? It looked like it was all the work of someone inside the organization, but he seriously doubted that. Anyone on the inside who knew these things would also know that the worst thing you could do to the boss was the double-cross. That meant you died and your whole family died. They just wouldn't take that chance. But, who?

As he was staring at the house and remembering the many times he had stayed there, enjoying the safety and seclusion from his daily world, he remembered often bringing his beloved son there for pleasant weekends. He also remembered a woman. It was the woman Dominic wanted to marry. Arty remembered that Dominic had dated her for a few months and really fallen hard for the bitch. The one he brought to this house where he intended to propose. It was the woman who laughed at his son and paid the price. After taking from her what she would have been expected to give in marriage, they had sent her away with the promise that one word of their actions would mean death to her and everyone she held dear. Now, Arty remembered more. Dominic told Arty that they did many things together and he really liked her company. He said he took her everywhere. Then, it hit Arty like a blow to the chest: *He took her everywhere!!!* Arty was suddenly consumed with anger, shock, and sadness. Oh, Dommy, he thought, you showed her everything, didn't you? She saw it all. She knew where our stores were. She's the one!

The plain brown van drove away. It was driven by a man who had started at the bottom as a simple hood and built an empire of crime. His mob name was somewhat undeserved. Yes, he had taken someone way out in the harbor and sunk him into the depths. But, it didn't go like the legend has it. The guy's name was Truppy Danos. He was a snitch. He was seen in an earnest conversation with a Trenton police detective and could no longer be trusted. It was supposed to go like the old days. They were going to take Truppy out in a boat, put his feet in a small tub of concrete, and push him over the side. But Arty made the mistake of saying they were going to put boots on the guy. The idiot that Arty sent to buy the tub didn't know the old way. He bought green garden boots, men's, extra-large. After giving his idiot soldier an ass-chewing and scathing ridicule, they made do with what they had. Truppy was a tall, skinny guy. They stuck his feet in the rubber garden boots and filled them with quick-dry cement while Truppy was begging and trying to explain. When the cement dried, they found that each boot weighed about forty pounds. Two guys couldn't pick up Truppy and the boots at the same time. So, while Truppy had a guy lifting each foot and Arty himself carrying a naked Truppy, they managed to get him over the side. Truppy was no dummy, as soon as he went under, he expelled all his breath and breathed in lungs full of dirty harbor water. He was dead before he hit bottom a hundred and ten feet down. Arty determined that this was the first and last time that he would ever do this. No matter. From then on, he was Arty Boots, the mobster who had put fifty men on the bottom of the harbor. Now because of this woman, he was himself back at the bottom. He was a wanted man. He was also now an angry, determined man on a deadly mission. It was simple. Find a certain woman and kill her slowly.

32

The pictures the authorities released with the "be on the lookout for" announcement showed a man with an average face, heavy beard, receding hairline, dimpled chin, nose wide at the bridge, and dark eyes. He was described as 5' 10" and of heavy build. Unfortunately, they were taken from the most recent photographs available of Arturo Donetti. The man who climbed the stairs and walked into the dance studio over Aaron Weaver's office looked nothing like that. He was a pleasant-looking, smiling, middle aged man in a nice tweed jacket over a button-down shirt and decent tie. He had a very neat Van Dyke beard and wore an English style fedora and expensive leather gloves. He stood smiling as he watched a lesson in progress. An attractive young woman in tights, a pink top, tutu, and ballet slippers was patiently showing a young girl how to hold her arms as she moved through a certain series of steps.

The instructor saw him and, smiling herself, approached the man. "Hello. Welcome to our studio. How can I help you?" It was Tommy's daughter, Laurie.

"Years ago, my daughter took instruction here. It was a very pleasant experience. I would like to contact the nice lady who taught her, but we have lost her name and number. I was wondering if you would have that information." Arty smiled again and waited.

The young instructor nodded. "It was funny that we never met her but feel like we know her anyway. When we took over the studio, we found many old records, so we know who she was."

Arty let nothing show on his face but felt a moment of triumph. He took a small note pad from his pocket along with a Mont Blanc ballpoint pen and prepared to write.

"Her name was Luna Norse. We think she was from Muncie, Indiana, wherever that is." She laughed. "I'm sorry, but that's all we know. That was from some old correspondence."

Arty thanked her graciously and went back down the stairs. He was tempted to go into the Battle just to look at it. He knew it was owned by the son of a bitch who had killed his son, but he was afraid that someone in there might recognize him in spite of his disguise. He was still going to get that bastard, but he wanted to find this woman first.

Revenge, Arty thought. It's all I have left. No son, no wife, no guys—I got nothing. And, it's all because of these two. His next move was a trip to Muncie, Indiana, wherever the hell that was. He was going to pay a visit to this Norse broad.

* * *

The drive was long but easy—almost all interstate. He was driving an ordinary, forgettable Chevy rental. After spending the night in a motel on I-70, he drove the last few miles into Muncie. It was a simple matter to find the Norse home in such a small burg.

It was the only one in the Muncie phone book. It was also easy to find out where the older Norse woman was. The neighbors were eager to help the distinguished gentleman who knew the Norse's from way back. Yes, it was so sad that Ivan had died so young and so sad that Ingrid had got the dementia. No, they did not know where the daughter was. She left several weeks ago and they have heard nothing of her whereabouts. Sorry. The son was nothing but trouble. He was somewhere in town. Nobody knew where. Sorry.

The distinguished gentleman's name was David Johnson. It was the identification taken from the body of the real David Johnson just before Arty killed him just one year ago. Johnson had defended himself against one of Arty's collectors and had to be punished. Before they buried him, Arty's crew had remarked at how much Johnson looked like Arty, so Arty had taken Johnson's license, credit cards, and family photos to hold just for an eventuality like this.

David Johnson walked into the lobby of the Lily Place Rest Home. It was with some difficulty that he did not visibly recoil at the odors that were invariably found in these places. Wearing the same clothes that put the dancer girl at ease, he approached the desk.

"Hello, there," said a smiling elderly woman at the desk. "How may we help you?"

Johnson smiled in return. "I wonder if I might be able to see Ingrid Norse? I'm visiting in the area and knew her and Ivan from long ago."

Shaking her head with a smile, "I am so sorry. We are unable to allow visitors to Mrs. Norse. She is in a very, ah, delicate condition with the need for constant care."

Johnson shook his head sadly and asked, "Is she able to communicate?"

"Oh, no. She is totally uncommunicative. She hasn't spoken a cogent word for at least two years."

Shaking his head in sadness, he asked, "Do you know where I might find Luna, the daughter?"

The woman laughed, "I wish we knew. She has been traveling God-knows-where for weeks now. She calls regularly to check on her mother's condition, but there's never a return number. I would be happy to relay a message the next time she calls."

"That would be very thoughtful." Johnson/Donetti paused while thinking. "Tell her that Dominic's dad was here visiting her mother. If you don't mind, add that I will also be visiting her brother." He took out a cell phone. "Would you take this number and give me a call when you hear something?"

"No problem. We can take care of that."

David Johnson made himself comfortable in Muncie, Indiana. He rented a suite at a local hotel where he enjoyed the free breakfast and evening happy hour. He guessed it would take maybe three or four days. He settled down to plotting how he could get out of the country after he was done.

It only took two.

* * *

Harp heard Norse scream. He had just decided to shave the beard and was standing at the mirror in his bathroom with scissors in hand. Assuming the worst, he grabbed a pistol off the stand next to his bed and ran through the suite to her room. He found Norse with shoulders bent forward and hands over her face gasping for breath.

"Luna, what the hell! What's wrong?" He was crouched, scanning the room.

Norse was gasping and took a moment to catch her breath. "He's there. He's in fucking Muncie!" Now she was screaming. "He's been to see my mother. He's going after my brother!"

Harp was confused. "Who's there!?" Harp put his hands on her shoulders, then with one hand, lifted her chin. "Calm down and tell me what's going on."

Norse took a deep breath and answered, "I called to check on my mother. You know I've been calling every couple of days—mostly just to be sure she's still alive."

"Yeah, I know. What happened?"

"Ethel said..."

Harp interrupted, "Who's Ethel?"

"Ethel is the sweet woman who works at the reception desk at Mom's nursing home. Norse took another deep breath and continued. "She said, 'There was a nice man here asking about your mother. He said to tell you he was Dominic's dad and he was going to go see my brother. He said he was looking forward to seeing me again.'"

Norse lifted her head and met Harp's gaze. Harp nodded and confirmed the unspoken question in her eyes, "He's figured it out." Harp shook his head slowly while in thought. "I should have known that he would eventually go down a list of all the people who might know the locations of the places we hit. Maybe even his own people didn't know *all* of those places. Probably the house gave him the answer. He remembered you being there with Dominic and put two and two together." He shrugged, "I'm sorry, Luna. I should have seen this coming."

"You know I've got to go back there, don't you?" She held his hands as she implored Harp for agreement.

"Yeah, I know. But, let's do some planning."

"What kind of planning? I go back and call the police, tell the story, and get some protection for me and my mother."

Harp shook his head. "It's not that simple, Luna. You would never be able to tell the police *why* this is happening. You have been involved in several felonies over the past few weeks. If you try to describe your relationship with Donetti, it would be impossible to leave out all that we have done."

Norse groaned and covered her face. "Harp, you know he will do anything to get even. He could kill my mother and brother. What am I supposed to do?"

"Okay. Let's look at the facts. He knows who you are. But, there's no way he could put you and me together. He wants me for something that's totally separate. Let's use that." Harp was pacing and thinking.

"Number one, it's time we got out of here anyway. We need to give the place back to Kip and all of us forget we've ever been here."

Norse was wringing her hands and listening intently. "You're coming with me?" she asked. "All the way to Muncie?"

Harp was surprised at the question. "Why, hell yes, Luna. I'm surprised you would even ask. This is as much my problem as yours."

With tears in her eyes, Norse pulled his head down and kissed a surprised Harp. "Thank you, thank you."

"Okay, first, let's get packing." For Norse it was easy. She put her clothes back in her suitcases. For Harp, it was more complicated. They still had all the guns taken from the gunsmith's shop–still in the large duffle. Then, they still had the millions in cash to do something with–now back in the backpack that he had carried away from Donetti's estate.

When they had everything together, they stood at the door looking around. Harp had texted Kip saying only *We're gone. Thanks. I owe you. Have the place CLEANED."* Kip would know what Harp meant: that is, carefully remove all signs that anyone other than Kip had been there.

With both heavily laden, they managed to take everything to Harp's Ford SUV in one trip. As always, it seemed to Harp, he was one traffic stop away from a long stay in prison. In this case, with all the guns and cash, Norse would be charged also. But, the gods of traffic stops remained kind. They drove directly to Harp's storage unit in Trenton where they left the guns and almost all the cash–some of the stuff was placed atop the old foot locker that had provided Harp with the vital tools to survive in another time. Boy, Harp thought, if ever this storage unit were broken into. It was in another person's name, though, and paid up for three more years.

33

It was dark when they headed west out of Trenton going to Muncie. They would arrive in the early morning. Ironically, they traveled the same roads that Arturo Donetti had driven days before. As Norse drove, they planned.

Harp laid out the bare bones of his plan. "Arty is expecting you. He's probably waiting for you. He is probably watching for you. He doesn't know about me. That's our wild card. We just have to figure out the best way to play it." Norse was listening intently. She understood that it was her very survival they were planning.

Harp continued. "You are going to arrive alone. You will be driving a rental car that we will pick up before we pull into Muncie." He thought for a minute, then asked, "Is there any way I can get into your house without being seen?"

Norse laughed, "Yes, there is an alley behind the house with tall fences around our back yard. My brother and I would walk close to the fences, which start right next to the door of the back porch. Neither our parents nor neighbors could see us slip out for some secret meetings with friends." She added, "The key is under the iron boot scraper. It's a long metal dachshund."

"Good. Do you have a garage, and is it enclosed?"

"Yes, it's a two-car garage. The doors open with a remote or with a keypad. My car is on one side and the other side is empty."

Harp thought some more as they rolled along the Interstate toward Indiana. "Here's what we'll do. You will stop somewhere where someone watching the house can't see us and let me out. I will go into your house the back way. You will then drive to your house, pull into the driveway, and then get out to hit the keypad. Quickly drive into the garage and quickly close the garage door. Act as if this is all normal."

Norse shuddered. "Oh, God, you think he will be watching when I do this?"

"I don't know, but we have to act like he is and be ready for anything."

It took some time to get the rental car. Harp left his car in a parking garage. Norse arrived at her house at 9 a.m., got out and punched the keypad, and drove her rental into the garage. She was careful not to scan the neighborhood as she activated the door and did her best to act casually. It was a bright, clear day. Each entered the house as planned with no problems. Harp was already inside and very careful to never be seen through any window. This was made easier by the old-fashioned curtains covering every window.

Harp helped her carry her suitcases into the house and brought his own small bag in. Once inside, they briefly hugged in relief in the kitchen and then both collapsed in chairs in the living room to prepare. Harp noticed that everything looked comfortable but dated. "Nice house," was all he could think of.

"It's pitiful, isn't it? This is where I grew up and I don't think I have changed a damned thing since. Every table, chair, bed, is just the way it was when I was a kid." She slouched with her hands in her pants pockets. "When I left for the big city, I thought I was gone forever. Then, when I came back from Trenton, I was so traumatized, it was all I could do to simply exist. Now, here we are, getting ready to do it all over again."

"But this time the outcome will be different," Harp observed. He looked at his watch, "What would you normally do after coming back from a long trip?"

"I guess I would gather up the mail, open the front door to just the storm door, maybe go out and sweep the porch, stuff like that."

"Okay. You do that and I'll be in here watching."

"You don't think he will do anything like from a distance?"

"No, he's not going to be that kind of shooter. Plus, he's going to want to say things and look at you when he pulls the trigger."

"Boy, that makes me feel a whole lot better," she said sarcastically.

Harp grinned. "Best I can do."

Norse did as Harp suggested. She opened the heavy wood door to leave just the windowed storm door closed. Then, she swept leaves off the porch and front steps and shook out the door mat.

Everything looked perfectly normal. And, that's what Arty thought as he watched through binoculars. He recognized her immediately. "Oh, the bitch is back in town," he sung to himself. Upon seeing her again, his plans changed on the spot. He was thinking back to when he and Dominic had so cruelly raped her. Now, he wanted to do that again. This time, however, she would not be allowed to walk away. He knew he would have to act fast.

He had already been in this pitiful burg too long. He needed to strike and run.

Harp and Luna watched the man get out of the car. He was wearing a very nice jacket and tie and a wool fedora with a feather in the band. He wore glasses, had a neatly trimmed beard, and was carrying a briefcase. He could easily be seen as an insurance or realty representative.

"Is that him?" Harp quietly asked from his position behind the door. He was armed with two weapons. He had a length of heavy metal pipe from the garage and a silenced nine that they had taken from the gunsmith's shop. He didn't want to shoot Arty immediately unless he had to.

"I don't know," she replied in an agonized whisper. Then when he got closer, she saw the telltale cruel set of his mouth and cold eyes, "It's him!"

"Okay, get in the kitchen and do like we planned. We still have to be sure."

Arty confidently strode up the steps and across the porch to ring the doorbell. As might happen in any small community, Norse came out of the kitchen wearing an apron and hollered, "Come on in, I'll be out as soon as I get this cake out of the oven!" Then she went back into the kitchen.

Arty smiled as he opened the door and walked into the living room thinking this was going to be much, much, easier than he could have imagined. He was reaching into his rear pants pocket when the pipe knocked him unconscious. Harp knew how hard to hit. He wanted him out but not dead...yet.

Arty regained consciousness while very solidly taped to a chair in the kitchen. Harp and Luna were quietly watching the process. Luna was now ninety-eight percent sure this was

Arturo Donetti. Removing the glasses and hat confirmed his identity.

They were discussing what to do with him now that they had him. Harp was careful to point out to Norse that Arty was probably wanted by Federal agencies and they could turn him in. Norse was silent as she listened.

"But he would still be alive, wouldn't he? He could still beat all these charges and be back out, couldn't he?"

Harp shrugged. "Yup. That could happen. These guys can pay for very expensive lawyers." Norse turned away.

Arty was listening. He started making sounds through the tape over his mouth and shaking his head. Harp removed the tape.

"Listen, we can forget all this. I give you guys a couple mil and we let bygones be bygones. Whattaya say?"

Harp couldn't resist. "I already got a couple mil from you when I blew up your house."

Donetti's eyes bulged, "You the fucker who did that?"

Harp continued. "Yeah, I was the one who was there when your idiot son was shot by one of your idiot hired helpers."

At this, Donetti went berserk. He began screaming. Harp put another piece of tape over his mouth.

Harp was turning around to find Norse when the first shot whipped past. Then there were two more in quick succession. The first hit Donetti in the right lung, the second in the stomach, and the third in the heart.

In total shock, Harp wheeled around to find Norse standing just eight feet away in the doorway with a small thirty-two revolver still pointed at her target. A very faint cloud of smoke was hanging in the air.

"JESUS, Luna! Goddam! I didn't want you to do that!" He easily took the pistol from her hand.

Norse said in a flat voice as if reciting, "It was my father's. He kept it in the pantry by the back door. He always said it was for snakes and possums. I didn't think it would work." She was staring at a very dead New Jersey mobster who had somehow ended up dead in a Muncie, Indiana, kitchen. Harp did not like the look in her eyes. He had seen it before. It told of a mind that was gone for now. Some came back, some didn't. Instead of shaking her, Harp wrapped his arms around her and stroked her hair. She just stood with arms hanging for many minutes, then she put her arms around Harp and cried with chest heaving gasps. He continued saying, "Okay, okay, okay." He knew she was crying out years of fear and shame.

Finally, Norse gently pushed him away and ripped paper towels off the nearby roll. When she finished blowing her nose and drying her face, she straightened her shoulders and said, "I have now shot two men to death and I do not regret either one. I am a murderer, executioner, a killer, a felon, and Lord knows what else. Obviously, what I am is NOT 'okay.'" Harp stood watching her as if she would disintegrate at any moment. She smiled and punched him gently in the chest and asked with some sarcasm, "Who's next?"

Harp was deeply appreciative that Norse was back. He really needed her. Arturo Donetti was very dead and he was a very big problem. Their planning had not gotten to the point of getting rid of a body. "Are there any places out in the boonies? You know, places where a body could just disappear?"

Norse tried to picture the area around Muncie where this could be done. "No, not around here. I can't think of anything."

But then, she cried out, "The mines! My grandfather worked in the coal mines."

Harp asked, "Coal? In Indiana?"

"There were some real deep mines right here. Most have shut down. There's one deep mine that closed decades ago after it had a collapse. It had several air shafts. The shafts are all supposed to be fenced off, but the fences are pretty much broken down. We used to go out there and throw rocks down the shafts just to see how long it took for them to reach bottom. They said those shafts go down some 200 feet."

"How close can we get with a car?"

"I don't know. It's been years since I went out there. I was just a kid. I think we would have to carry him a long way." She glanced at Donetti and shuddered again. She did not want to touch him. She felt that, even in death, he was somehow poisonous. "There's one I kind of remember that had a road near it."

"Are there houses around these shafts?"

"Lord, no. That's all coal company property.

"Could you find it in the dark?"

"Maybe with a flashlight. The trail up to the shaft starts right next to an old school bus stop."

Harp sat in a chair next to Donetti thinking. Norse waited.

"All right, we're going to have to do this in several steps. The first thing is to get him undressed."

Norse almost lost it. She bent forward with her face in her hands shaking her entire body in repugnance at the thought of touching the body.

Harp explained. "He was seen arriving. He has to be seen leaving. I'll wear his clothes and drive off in his car. Before that, though, we'll bundle him up in garbage bags and put him into the trunk of your rental. You'll leave shortly after I do. I'll take his car to some rental place that's closed and leave it with the keys in it. It doesn't matter which one. They'll take care of it. We'll then go together to this mine place and dump this piece of shit in a hole where he belongs."

Norse listened carefully saying "My God" over and over. She then nodded and they got to work.

Donetti hadn't bled much thanks to the shot to the heart. His shirt and tie had bullet holes, but the rest was intact. Without thinking, Harp read the information in the wallet. "So, we have Mr. David Johnson, from Newark, New Jersey." Harp knew it was a fake ID. Norse didn't. Harp heard her head hit the door of a cabinet on the way to the floor. After reviving her with washcloths soaked in iced water, he made her look closely at the picture on the license. It was very obviously *not* Arturo Donetti. It was close enough for a casual glance but that's all.

"Oh God, I thought I killed the wrong man." She took the cloth and held it to her face. "I can't take much more of this, Harp. I really can't."

Harp took the cash from the wallet and asked, "Do you have a shredder?"

"In the office." She pointed. Harp shredded everything. The empty wallet would be found on the roadside.

Harp helped her to her feet and held her for a moment. She was seriously trembling. Harp hoped she wasn't going into shock. "Come on. We've got just a few more things to do."

In the dusk of the day, the man who had entered Norse's house hours before came out wearing the same clothes (unless closely inspected) and with a neatly trimmed beard and jaunty fedora. His trousers appeared to be too short and the jacket quite tight. He went to his car and drove off. Shortly thereafter, Norse left her garage and she, too, drove off.

Harp left the car and the keys at the first closed auto rental place they found and got in with Norse. With some hesitancy, she eventually drove close to where the trail was supposed to be. "This doesn't seem right. I know it was right here. There!" She pointed at an overgrown dirt road branching off.

"Drive up this track as far as you can and cut the lights."

Harp dragged Donetti's body from the trunk, then draped Donetti's clothes over all the reflective surfaces on the back of the car. Harp was now back in his usual attire.

With great difficulty, Harp hoisted the mobster's body over his shoulder and told Norse to lead the way. It took a lot longer than either of them expected. He had to stop and rest several times. Finally, they came to the rusted gate that said No Trespassing. Around the sides of the gate, the chain link fences had fallen to the ground.

"Be careful, Harp. Here it is. It was a good thing she was leading the way because Harp couldn't see anything. He was expecting a yawning chasm, a large black hole. This was just a depression in thick grass, until you were on top of it and could see the blackness.

"That's it?" he asked with some serious doubt.

"It's a lot bigger than it looks, so stay back away from the edge." She tossed a large rock into the depression and said, "Listen." Harp could hear the rock bounce from side to side. The sound became weaker and weaker and then, after about five seconds, there was a quiet, distant click.

"Holy shit!" Harp had heard things fall from high places before but never like this.

Norse grinned, "I told you. It is really deep."

Now Harp was very respectful of this abyss because you couldn't see exactly where the edges were. He carefully laid Donetti's body on solid ground next to the opening. He then sat on the ground and pushed him through the grass and over the edge with his feet. They listened as Donetti bounced and careened off the walls to a far-off dull thump when he landed. But that was followed by a clatter as what sounded like a large amount of other rock and soil came loose and fell down the shaft atop the body. Arturo Bignelli Donetti was thus entombed for eternity among the rotting and skeletal remains of other animals that had also fallen to the bottom of an abandoned ventilation shaft near Muncie, Indiana. Only two people knew of the ultimate fate of this once feared mobster, and that secret would die with them.

Those same very tired people got out of the car in Norse's garage. It was late. The first thing they did was make sure there was no sign that Johnson/Donetti had been there. The next thing they did was go to bed. They were in the same bed because they were both too tired to care. It was still dark when Norse woke Harp and said in a tight voice, "Make love to me." Harp was more than happy to oblige. It had been a long time for him, too. He found that Norse was somehow desperate in her lovemaking. She was trying too hard. He felt like asking her to slow down, quit the frantic pushing and grasping. They had grown close and he truly cared for her. This wasn't the way he wanted it to happen. He finished. She didn't. Neither was happy with the result. They were quiet afterward, both deep in thought.

"That was all wrong, wasn't it, Harp?"

"Yeah," Harp responded quietly.

"I didn't want it to be that way either. It was like I was forcing myself to like it."

Harp understood. "You were using me to escape what they had done to you. You were getting back at those guys." Harp turned on his side to face Norse. "It's never going to be right if you do it that way. I'm tired." He rolled away from her and went back to sleep. She was hurt by his words but knew he was right.

Harp was still asleep when he felt Norse's hands stroking his face, then his chest, then lower. It was early morning, gray light in the windows. He opened his eyes and looked at her with eyebrows raised in question.

"Let's try again," she said.

"You sure?"

"Yes." She smiled. "You lead the way."

It was much better. It was the way it was supposed to be. They took turns leading the way. Later, Norse got up with a smile and a sense of completeness she hadn't felt in years. The fear was gone. She was exalting to herself, "I can do this now."

Over a bland breakfast of old, microwaved muffins and instant coffee, they nibbled and sipped before facing a truth each knew was coming. "You know I can't go back there with you," Norse said very softly while looking directly into Harp's eyes. "I have to stay here. I have to take care of Mom and my little shitheel brother."

Harp nodded. "I guess I knew that. And, you know I can't stay here. My whole life, everything I own, my history, it's all in Trenton; plus, there's still a bunch of stuff I have to take care of."

It was her turn to nod. "It is funny, isn't it, what life does. You and I have been through so much together, been so close, yet we will most likely never see each other again. I know I will

be happy if I never see Trenton again for the rest of my life."
She was smiling with shining eyes and tears on her cheeks. She
rose from her chair and came around the table to stand next to
Harp where she pulled his head against her breasts. Harp held
her in return, saddened by what he knew was coming. "I love you
because of your courage. I love you for showing me what a real
man is and for what you did for me. You set me free. I think I
can lead a normal life now. Maybe find someone I can trust with
my feelings. I will always love you—but not in a way that would
hold us together. Please say you understand that."

Harp answered slowly as he tried to describe his own feelings. "I understand because I feel the same way. The memories I
have with you are the kind that will stay with me for the rest of
my life." They remained holding each other, knowing that when
they parted, it would be forever.

Finally, Harp gently removed her arms from around his head
and said, "Hey, you need to drive me back to my car! I'm going
to hit the road back to good old Trenton! I've got some businesses to run!" He was sounding loudly jocular just to keep from
tearing up himself. Stoicism in the face of loss was a necessary
warrior attribute he had learned the hard way. "I will be coming
back to life in Trenton and I expect it's going to be complicated."

34

Harp drove from Muncie to Trenton by way of Goldsboro, North Carolina. When he left Luna Norse, he felt like one chapter in his life had ended and a new one had begun. With this beginning, his loyalty to his squad demanded that they be totally informed and brought up to date. The best way to do that would be to go directly to that beautiful North Carolina farm now owned by two of the men who had had his back through all the shit handed down by Adam Willarde and now Arturo Donetti. He wasn't sure if he could tell Bonny and Weeks everything. Check that; he knew he *could* tell them everything, but he didn't know if it would be good for them to know *all* that he had done. He had called and told them he was coming. They were excited and said they would get in touch with Kip who would fly in. Harp was excited also. He had learned to love these guys and, more than that, he trusted them without reservation. What greater thing can you say about a person, Harp thought, than to say you trust and respect him?

Once again on the country's fabulous Interstate System, he made it from Muncie to Winston-Salem where he ran out of gas figuratively and literally. In paying cash for a room, he was reminded of the millions of dollars sitting in a bag in a storage locker in Trenton. He had no idea what the hell he was going to do with it. So, oddly, in this modern world, it was becoming more and more difficult to spend good old American cash. You could spend a little, deposit a little, or carry a little, but large amounts caught the attention of the banks and invited the attention of the IRS. Norse would get a check for roughly a half million dollars for her house and a small twelve-acre piece of farm land her father had owned on the outskirts of Muncie. The sales agreement would stipulate that she had lifetime use of both, with the taxes paid by the new owner. Harp would have to work out a legal way to repay Kip.

Harp made the last few miles in about three hours and arrived at the farm around noon. He was impressed with the appearance of everything along the long drive from the main road to the farm headquarters. The fields, fences, hedges, and crops showed great care. He felt a deep of sense of pleasure that these two warriors, without a bit of experience in agriculture, had made this dream such a nicely-done reality.

He pulled into the large area between the house and the barns, noticing the perfectly cut grassed area inside the picket fence. Toward the barns was a confusion of machinery, most of which he had no idea what they were used for. Golf carts, motorcycles, tractors, pickups, and one mean looking monster that had long pointed things sticking out of the front. Harp couldn't believe that these city guys, these incredible soldiers, his squad, knew how to operate this stuff. He was standing there shaking his head when he heard a roar from the house and three men in various kinds of dress ran down the steps and through the gate. They began alternately hugging and pummeling Harp while calling him profane names and threatening to kill his ass if he ever pulled this shit again. He wasn't sure what this shit was, but he agreed to never do it again anyway. After he had been thoroughly and roughly welcomed, they all stopped and studied one another with big smiles. Harp was still not back to his normal appearance. He had longish bushy hair and the graying Van Dyke beard that Norse had created. The scars on his head were less evident but studied nonetheless. He studied each of them in return.

Bonny was first to speak. "Goddam, Sarge, the last time I saw you, I really, honest-to-God didn't think you were going to make it. You look pretty damned good, considering."

Amid the laughter, Weeks chimed in. "Yeah, when Bonny told us what had happened in the hospital and how you looked when Kip picked you up, we just kept saying our old Sarge is too damned tough to die. But then we would say, 'How can anybody take two fucking rounds to the back of the head and live?'"

Then Kip added, "No shit. When I got you up to Philly, I was surprised that you were still alive. I still don't know how we got you upstairs and into bed still breathing. You were no shit dead but somehow not dead yet."

Harp held up his hands just to slow everything down. "Hold it. Hold it, dammit." He looked each of them in the eye as they stood silent. "The only reason I made it was because of you guys. There were times when I wasn't sure myself, but I knew I couldn't let you down. That kept me going."

He turned to Kip. "Kip, giving me that place to hide out and recuperate is something that I can never pay you enough for."

"Bonny, you saved my life in that hospital. How do I thank you for that?"

Weeks was looking slightly left out. "Weeks, none of this could have happened if you didn't have Bonny's back. You had ALL of our backs. It was ALL of you who kept me alive. Thank you, thank you." This time he did something which was very uncharacteristic for the hardened old soldier. He went and hugged each of them then looked into their eyes and nodded.

Bonny, stated, "Okay, Sarge, it's time for a total debriefing. We have got to know what all happened. So much shit went down that we don't know about. It's time to fill us in."

Harp nodded. "You're right, Bonny. But, it's a long story with some things you're just going to have to trust me on. You all remember the old need-to-know regs. That kind of applies here. There's some things you just don't need to know."

Harp had started to explain more when all three listeners directed their attention to something behind him. He turned to see a very attractive woman approaching the gate. She came through and confidently walked up to stand next to Weeks. She smiled and extended her hand to Harp "Now I finally get to meet the famous Sgt. Harp Harper, the man who rescued my Felipe."

Bonny and Kip smiled. Weeks had suddenly turned into an awkward teenager in love. They were holding hands. "Sarge, this is my wife, Maria Rodrigues Gonzales Weeks. We've been married for two months."

Bonny butted in, "And we have hardly seen Weeks for two months."

They laughed as Weeks explained. "Sarge, we wanted to wait for you to come back. It was so long and we just didn't know and we really, really wanted to get married."

Harp said, "Weeks, if you *had* waited for me to show up

and not married this beautiful woman, I would have been very angry and disappointed. You showed uncommon good sense to go ahead. I congratulate both of you. I'm sorry I missed the wedding."

Weeks was relieved. "Thanks, Sarge. That means a lot to both of us."

Harp needed to get the squad alone somewhere and talk. "Guys, I want to say hello to Fart. Who will come with me?"

Bonny jumped in. "Let's all take the four-wheeler and run out there."

Maria sensed that this was something that the men wished to do alone. "You all go ahead. I have a lot to do here. I can see this dog Fart any time." She smiled, kissed Weeks, and pushed him away.

While they rode through the fields, Harp and Kip were asking questions about the farm's operation. Both were impressed with the work of Bonny and Weeks. Once at the grave site, they stood in silence remembering what a dog named Fart had done for all of them. Then they all flopped on the grass in the shade while Harp told them the whole story. Almost. He left out the actual acts of killing. They didn't need to know that Norse had taken the lives of two men, one of whom was Donetti. They didn't need to know about Booge and Frat Boy. They laughed at Harp's description of blowing out the bottom of the house. They whistled when Harp told them how much money was in there and how much he had taken. He added that they could have any of it they wanted. They laughed again when he gave details of shooting up the pasta restaurant. They whistled at the nerve of Harp and Norse in stealing all the weapons. Harp left out the part about shooting the guys who came in while they were still there. He said he was going to dump the stuff. He concluded that he was ready to get on with his life. To the men who were listening, it sounded like Harp felt he was no longer threatened.

Weeks asked the question, "Well, what about Arty Boots? "

Bonny asked, "And what about the guy who took a shot at you in the hospital?"

Harp said nothing. He just looked into the eyes of each of them in turn.

They all got it. They knew his capabilities. Kip asked, "Both?"

Harp nodded.

Smiling, Bonny observed, "So now you can go back to good old Trenton and pick up where you left off months ago."

Harp grinned back. "Yep. Now that I've seen you guys, that's exactly what I'm going to do."

35

Driving back into Trenton was an emotional experience for Harp. It was too damned often in his life that he was forced to leave what had always been his home base. He was telling himself that this time, by God, nothing was ever going to make him depart his favorite city. He was just plain tired when he finally opened the door to his condo. He didn't bother checking his mail box knowing that it would be jammed full of junk. He never got much anyway. Nothing had been touched inside and everything still worked through the wonder of automatic deductions for water, cable, and electricity. Leaving all that he carried on the floor by the door and the clothes he was wearing on the floor by the bed, he crawled under the covers and slept. For once, it was dreamless and deep.

Waking to a new day, the first for many months without the threat of ambush, Harp lay in bed for a long time planning the next steps in his coming back to life for the people in his small sphere in Trenton. He knew his appearance had changed—and it wasn't for the better. The scar on his forehead was very obvious, as were the scars showing through the hair on the back and side of his head. As usual, he didn't give a rat's ass how he looked. He knew he had some explaining to do.

The Battle would be first. He really wanted to know how it had done in this absence. He wanted to see Tommy and Lew. Harp surprised himself with the next objective. He wanted to get his new establishment up and running. He was now even more determined to carry out his plan on how it would be designed and operated. This new approach was totally different from what he had originally planned. One thing for sure—money was not a problem. In fact, money *was* a problem. He had a few million dollars in untraceable cash sitting in a bag in his storage locker, and he did not yet know how to use it. The only thing he did know was that he was going to try to give most of it away. He planned that the Vet LZ would play a role in this.

Harp walked into the Battle a little before three while Lew and Tommy were huddled over the receipts for the morning business. Deep in discussion, neither looked up at first. Lew was the first to turn around. His mouth dropped open and he hit Tommy on the arm. Tommy jumped and scowled at Lew, then he turned to look at the person who just entered. Harp walked to his favorite stool at the end of the bar and said, "What's it take for a man to get a drink in this place?"

With the first actual wide smile Harp had ever seen on Tommy, showing a mouth full of crooked teeth, the stocky ex-boxer went directly to Harp's bottle and poured him a double.

Harp said, "Pour one for yourself and one for Lew."

Tommy hesitated but did as he was told. "Boss, I never drink on the job. This is my first and my last."

Lew said, "I ain't never had a shot of fifteen-dollar whisky and ain't hardly never had one at three."

Each tossed his drink and slammed the glass on the bar. It was a sound that seemed to punctuate the importance of the moment. They stood in contented silence for a few seconds.

Then Lew said, "Damn, Mr. Harper, when we heard what happened, then when we didn't hear what more happened, we all figured you were laid up somewhere and maybe even seriously deceased." Harp had gotten used to Lew's manner of speaking and even understood him most of the time.

Harp smiled, happy to be back in his favorite hangout. "Well, I survived, as you can tell, and I am back and ready to get back to work." Then he added with a kind tone, "And I really do not see where it would do any good to talk about everything that happened to me. I want to just forget about it."

They nodded in solemn agreement. Tommy said, "Let's get Neal to bring you up to date. He's back in the office doing something." Then quietly, Tommy added. "He's doing a hell of a job. You wouldn't believe the kind of business we're doing." Then he yelled, "Hey, Neal. The boss is back in town."

Neal came limping out of the office with a huge grin and handshake for Harp. "Glad to see you back, Mr. Harper. I'm happy to report that everything is in order, all bills are paid, all permits and licenses up to date, and you've got a sizable amount in the bank." Tommy and Lew grinned with pride.

For a normal business owner, all this would have been very good news. But for Harp, all it did was confirm that the Battle was truly lost forever. It was no longer the kind of dark, quiet, hangout that he wanted. But he laughed and expressed enthusiasm with the rest of them and they were happy. He merely said, "Thanks, Neal. We'll get into the details later."

Excited voices at the door announced the entrance of the

young ladies running the dance studio. Then, behind them was the tall, quiet presence of Aaron Weaver. The crowd gathered around Harp, and he fielded the mostly gentle questions and expressions of relief that he had returned. Harp sensed in all of them an effort to see the scars. He would turn his head to see eyes quickly drop away from probing looks at his scalp and forehead. He supposed he would just have to get used to it.

Harp was tempted to settle in and have a few more drinks, but he knew the word would spread fast and there was a telephone call that he had to make before this word got to a certain female lawyer. He first thought of calling from the office, but then realized with a certain sadness that it was really no longer *his* office. Amidst exuberant expressions of joy at having him back, Harp left the Battle. He needed to call in the privacy of his condo.

"Sandra Kowalski, please." Harp had dialed the number after thinking carefully about what he would say. He was standing somewhat nervously in his own kitchen.

After the call was relayed, she answered. "Kowalski here."

"Hi, Kowalski, I…"

She recognized his voice immediately. "So it's just 'Hi Kowalski'?" with great disbelief.

"I…" Harp was going to try to explain.

"You bastard. I see your head blown to pieces in the hospital and I think you're going to die and I am so scared. And it's 'Hi Kowalski' after three months with not one friggin' word."

"I couldn't…" Harp wanted to explain why it was safer for her not to know.

"You couldn't call or send a goddamned note? Maybe tell one of those killer buddies of yours to talk to good old Kowalski?"

"Kowalski, it was…"

"Then you disappear and nobody knows whether you're dead or alive and I think you are most likely dead, and now you show up with 'Hi Kowalski'?" Her voice rose in pitch and volume until she was nearly screaming at the end of the question.

By now Harp had forgotten that he felt he had been right not to let her know where he had been hiding. She always did this to him. How, he wondered, could he always be wrong? He tried again. "Dammit, Kowalski, I felt it was safer for you if you didn't know. I knew they would try again. I just didn't want them to think of you as a way to get to me." Harp took a deep breath of relief at having finally gotten it out.

This calmed her down a bit. "Harp, I am not a child. I don't need a friggin' shot up old army rat to be my nanny."

"I know. Maybe I should have kept you in the loop. I had to do what I thought was best."

"Well, are you okay now? Those wounds to your head seemed so bad. I don't see how you can survive wounds like that and then just go back to normal function."

"Yeah, everything is back to normal except for the new scars. Plus, and I haven't shared this with anyone else, I sometimes have a little trouble with simple math. Columns of numbers get confusing a little." He paused. "But that's getting better."

"Well, gee, you get shot in the head twice and one of those shots smacks a metal plate in your miserable skull where you already have had serious cerebral trauma. Can anyone guess why you might have a few cognitive issues?"

Harp laughed. "When you put it that way, I guess I should expect it." Harp had escaped the hospital before the usual counseling that would have been provided for such head wounds. They would have told him what to expect.

"And, another thing, Harper, what's changed? Why suddenly show up for all the world to see? How do we know they won't try again?" This was a question that Harp had not anticipated. He suddenly realized that he had to continue to act like he was still a target. He could not act like there was no threat from Donetti. That could mean only one thing to those who knew him and his capabilities. His silence as he grappled with this realization was taken the right way by Kowalski–which, of course, was the exact wrong way for Harp's good.

In an ominous tone, she said, "You did it again, didn't you, Harper? There was a threat, and the incredible Sgt. Horace Harp Harper makes the threat disappear." She was referring to the former Adam Willarde who had threatened to kill her and her family. Willarde had died on a golf course from a shot taken hundreds of yards away. The killer had never been found. Harp was proud of that shot. Kowalski was furious that he had done it for her.

"No, no, nothing like that. It's been weeks now and I figure he just gave up on me. I have to live my life the way I want to. I can't walk around thinking about this all day."

"Sure, Harper." She was not convinced.

Hesitantly, Harp asked, "Is there any chance we could get together, Kowalski?" This was not what he really wanted to know and Kowalski sensed it.

There was a long pause. "I think for now, the answer is no. I have a lot of big memories with you, Harp, and right now they are not coming together very well. Maybe sometime later. Bye."

Harp put the phone down. He was happy that she had said "sometime later." And, as usual, he felt that he had done everything wrong when it came to Sandra Kowalski.

36

First on Harp's list of priorities was to get his new business up and going. He had an idea and didn't know if it would work, but he wanted to try. The goal had two parts. He wanted to do something for other veterans, and he wanted to get rid of a large amount of cash. He figured that a good way to do both was to own a bar that lost money due to poor management. The poor management would be the result of an overly generous credit policy. That's the kind of place the Vet LZ would be.

Harp was at the new building when he called the realtor/ attorney J.D. Elliott, who had represented Edgar Priest in the sale of this property. Harp wanted recommendations for the renovations he planned. He was puzzled by the tone of Elliott's voice when he answered Harp's call. Elliott angrily said he would be right over because he sure as hell wanted to talk to Harp.

Harp was standing in the old kitchen looking out at the layout of the Vet LZ when he heard loud banging on the front door. He opened the door for Elliott, who roughly pushed past Harp then turned and pointed a finger at him. Harp scowled but held his temper. He definitely did not like to be pushed.

"What the hell were you thinking, driving Ed up there to Rochester! He didn't ever have to go up there again. His god-damned family hated him! If I had taken him, I would have, by God, brought him back!"

Harp suddenly understood Elliott's anger. He backed away with hands up and tried to explain. "Mr. Elliott, in the first place, for me, the trip to Rochester was just part of the sales agreement. Secondly, I did not know what he planned until I let him out at the cemetery. Even then, it was just an instinct that something was up. He never told me what he was going to do and, frankly, what he did in that cemetery was his business."

"You could have stopped him. You could have talked him out of it." Elliott was less angry.

Harp was being very patient because he could see Elliott's pain at the loss of his old friend. "I don't know if you understand this, but even when I understood what he was going to do, I felt that it was his right. I have seen too many men die. I have seen many men die just because they wanted to. When a person comes to that point, when death looks better than life, there really isn't much anyone can do."

Elliott's shoulders slumped. More quietly, he said, "I know, dammit. But we've known each other for forty-some years. It really hurts that he would want to die like that without sharing at least the thought of it with me."

They stood silently, Elliott rubbing his face and looking at the floor. Finally, he shook his head as if to shake away an unpleasant image. He asked, "All right. To hell with that. You called about something. What was it?"

"It's okay if you don't want to get involved, but I need to know the names of some really good people who can do some major renovations on this place. I thought that, in your business, you might have some ideas."

"Yeah, I have a couple of very good contacts who would need some work. I'll have them call you." He looked around with this new information in mind. "Gonna bring the place up to date, huh?"

"Yeah, I've got some ideas that I want to try. It's gonna take some big changes. I want to make the place especially suited for veterans. It's gonna be the Vet LZ."

Elliott was surprised. "Really? You know, Ed and Hal would kind of like that. I hope it works out. Yeah, I'll be glad to help."

Harp was elated that the first steps had been taken. One of the changes Harp planned was the complete renovation of the upstairs space. He was going to move from his condo to live in the large apartment over the bar. It was crazy to be paying for the condo when he had this space available.

* * *

Once the work started, the news spread quickly. Within two weeks it seemed like the entire city knew what he was doing. This brought some welcome and some unwelcome attention. The welcome attention was the number of veterans who applied for jobs. The unwelcome attention came from the final attempt on his life brokered by the now deceased Arturo Donetti.

Harp was in the process of moving basic living items into the upstairs apartment. It wasn't done yet, but it was almost livable. He had parked behind the store and brought things up the kitchen stairway. On this one fateful night, he had decided to stay the night rather than drive back to his condo. He was asleep on the one usable bed, and there were no lights. Outwardly, the building looked empty as usual.

Part of the renovation project involved installation of new wiring up and down. He followed the recommendation of the electricians and included communications between the up and down floors of the building. Now there was an intercom system with mics in the bar and kitchen. Eventually, there would be cameras that would show him at the flick of a switch what was going on in his downstairs establishment. Harp had debated with himself on whether this was unfair surveillance or just good business. In any case, on this night, the intercom had not been turned off. The cameras and monitors weren't hooked up yet.

Harp was awakened by the familiar small squeak made by opening the front door. It took mere seconds for his mind to return to combat mode. He had spent years being awakened by sounds that could mean his life or the life of his men were at risk. It was 3 a.m. and somebody was in the bar. Barefoot, in shorts and tee shirt, with his favorite Sig nine, Harp eased down the kitchen stairs and moved with no sound to the kitchen door. The weak yellow light from the street outside showed a figure of a large man crouching behind the bar. Harp simply said, "Hey." The figure straightened and turned toward Harp. Reasoning that a person found in this situation would necessarily be armed, Harp shot the figure. His shot struck the man in the left shoulder, neatly breaking the humorous. The shock of it drove the man to his knees on the floor behind the bar. Harp did not know how badly the man was wounded and quickly moved closer, ready to shoot again. The man was on his knees but trying to turn again. Harp rushed closer and kicked the man with a heel to the side of the head, which left him unconscious.

After checking to make sure he was out, Harp dragged the man from behind the bar and bound his hands behind his back with electrician's tape from a worker's tool belt and his feet with his belt. Turning on the small under bar light, Harp saw what the man had been doing. He had not finished putting a small explosive object with a telephone actuator on a utility shelf under the drain board. Years of service in the sandpit made Harp familiar with this type of explosive, so he easily disarmed it. He searched the person's clothes and found the matching telephone, keys, and a wallet. He also found a Sig nine in a shoulder holster and a 25-caliber automatic in an ankle holster.

The man moaned as Harp dragged him to the end of the bar and propped him up. Harp pulled a chair over and watched as the guy came around. The wallet info said the guy's name was Donald Trask. He was a big guy, about six two. Curly dark hair. He had a big head but with small eyes and long hooked nose over a strange small mouth with no lips. His eyes were squinted and his mouth was twisted in pain. In the dim ambient light, he looked almost grotesque.

Finally, Trask looked at Harp, looked around the room, looked at the belt around his ankles, then finally at the bomb on the floor next to Harp. "You found it, huh." He groaned and tried shifting to ease the pain in his arm which, broken or not, was pulled behind his back.

"Yup. It wasn't hard. Easy to disarm, too. Seen 'em before."

Trask nodded. "Could I have some water? I'm really dry."

"Sure." Harp drew some tap water and put a straw in it. He said, "If you move anything but your mouth, I will shoot you in your other arm." Harp held the glass as Trask drank and did not move a muscle.

Trask groaned again. "I think you broke my arm. What was it?"

"Just a nine. Hollow tip."

"That'll do it."

Harp got right to the point. "Who paid you?"

"Hell, you know who paid me."

"I got an idea but want to hear it."

"Arty Boots."

Harp nodded. "I heard he had the entire Federal government on his ass and he disappeared."

"Yeah. But he paid me up front, and I wanted to get the job done before he gets back. He's a mean son-of-a-bitch when you don't finish a job."

Harp smiled, shook his head, and waited.

It took a while for the head shake to register, but then Trask's eyes widened, "You got 'im?" Harp shrugged. Trask shook his head in disbelief. "We tried to reason with Arty. We all knew that when they braced you and Dominic got killed, it was a total fuckup by Booge and Whip." Trask added, "He didn't know that he was up against a fuckin' pro."

"I am not a pro. I am just a damned soldier who doesn't like being threatened. How many of you are still out to get me?" Harp did not expect an answer. Trask surprised him.

"I'm all that's left. Somebody shot up our meeting place and everybody else is either in a wheelchair, in custody, or dead." Harp was gratified at the unintended consequences of that escapade. Trask continued, "Without Arty, the whole organization has gone to shit. The other guys across the river are picking up the pieces trying to put something back together."

"Are those 'guys across the river' interested in me, too?"

"Fuck no, they don't know about you and couldn't care less anyway. If they knew you did it, they'd pat you on the back and try to hire you."

Harp was considering options, "So, I get you to the hospital and they make you better, you would do a little time, and then probably end up working for the other guys." He casually added, "You probably got a good rep for doing this dirty work and they would take you on. Right?"

Trask's face brightened with the notion that Harp would take him to a hospital. With some pride, he responded, "Yeah, I probably would. I got a solid record for taking care of things. You know, it's just business as usual. Guys need to know there are consequences if they get out of line."

"And the consequence is usually fatal?"

Trask tipped his head to the side and repeated, "It's just business."

Sitting in the darkness, Harp felt even more darkness in the presence of this man. "You know, I've killed a lot of people, but they were all trying or had tried to kill me. What does it take to kill people for the simple reason that they didn't pay a few bucks or do something some mob boss asshole wanted them to do?"

Trask winced as he shifted again. "The whole world is a crooked place. It's all about money. It always has been. The little guys pay the big guys. So what? There ain't nothing else. Whoever got the money, got the power. You want to make any money, you work for the ones who got the power."

The simplicity was chilling to Harp. "And, if I call the cops and they come and take you in, you go up for a couple of years because you got slick lawyers and they would argue that you didn't actually do anything here. The fact that I stopped you would count in your favor. In fact, the way things are today, they might charge me with excessive force and put *me* in jail."

Trask laughed at the truth of it. "Ain't this modern world wonderful."

"What was the plan for this?" Harp held up the explosive package. "Outside of the obvious."

Trask put on his most earnest face, "I was going back to my car, get a couple miles away, then blow it."

"A couple miles away you couldn't see if anyone was in here or not, could you?"

"I, ah, would assume it's empty."

Harp's recent experience with explosives had taught him well. "That's bullshit. This would take the whole building down. You didn't come here to ruin a business, you came here to blow up my ass, and, if anyone else happened to be in here, murder them too."

Trask stared at the ceiling rather than deny the obvious. He very casually asked, "When you gonna call the cops? I need to get this arm treated."

Harp was thinking. He had concluded that there was no way to let this guy go back to his dirty work, but what were his options? Mainly, he was the last link in the Donetti-Harper chain of events. If he were gone, then it was truly over–but, only if he were gone. Harp made up his mind.

"Trask, roll over on your stomach." Trask quickly complied. "I'm going to cut the tape on your wrists, then I want you to roll back over and take the belt off your ankles." After the tape was cut, Trask rolled onto his back and sat up with another loud groan as his left arm flopped loosely. He clumsily removed the belt with one hand. "Now stand up." Harp backed away with his

Sig aimed at Trask's head. Trask was trembling, and his face was very pale as he struggled to his feet. Harp noted with relief that all the bleeding had been confined to Trask's clothes.

"No need to worry, Harper, I don't even know if I can walk."

"Take your time." Harp got behind Trask and grabbed the collar of his jacket. Trask was holding his left arm and stumbling as Harp turned him and walked him back down behind the bar. Harp pushed Trask to the point near the sink where he had first seen him. Harp let go and backed away.

Trask turned back toward Harp with a puzzled look on his face. He saw the gun and the look on Harp's face. It was the cold flat stare empty of all mercy and understanding. That would have described his own face many times just before he pulled the trigger. His shoulders slumped at the realization of what was coming. He had always felt that it would end this way. No condo in Belize.

He said, "Do what you gotta do." And Harp did it.

37

The police and EMTs were there within minutes after Harp's call. When you get a 911 saying a man's been shot inside a bar at 4 a.m., the adrenaline surges and you hit the lights. Then you get to race through empty city streets as fast as you can drive and leap from the vehicle with weapons drawn. The first officers were actually disappointed when they arrived at the scene of the purported crime. The front door to Ed and Hal's was open, the lights were on, and some guy wearing a tee shirt and chinos was sitting in a chair away from other chairs and tables. There was a desert tan Glock locked open with clip removed on a table many feet away from the man.

Harp pointed and said, "He's behind the bar. Don't touch the package on the bar or the cell phone." He pointed at the table. "That Glock over there is mine." They saw only a tightly wrapped brick-sized object with wires and a cell phone resting on the bar beside it. They approached it anyway until they were satisfied the guy wasn't lying. Then they backed off and got back on their radios. This changed everything. One cop walked to the end of the bar and looked at the floor behind it. Trask was lying face up in that narrow space, very dead, with an arm lying diagonally over his face with the hand holding an automatic. Again, there was more excited radio activity.

Following procedure, they cuffed Harp and put him in the back of a patrol car out front. He had done this before. He knew the drill. He made himself as comfortable as possible, rested his head on the back of the seat, closed his eyes, and waited. He was satisfied that his actions would be found justified and even more satisfied that the thing with Donetti would be finally, totally finished. About a half hour later, Harp was almost asleep when Detective Jay Carroll opened the car door. He leaned down and smiled. "We meet again, Mr. Harper. I find it, um, interesting that you're still alive." Carroll told one of the officers to help Harp out of the car and remove the cuffs. He walked him back into the building to one of the tables and told him to sit and don't move.

The explosives package and phone were gone. The body was still there. The techs were busy taking photographs, making drawings, dusting, and measuring. Harp's desert Glock was confiscated. Carroll came back to the table and sat across from Harp. He looked even more tired than Harp remembered from before. Without preamble, he started, "We know who he is and we know who you are. Now we need to know what the hell happened." He laid his recorder on the table, cited the circumstances, and pushed the record button. "Why don't you tell me what happened. Start from the beginning, and don't leave anything out."

So Harp told him exactly what happened—sort of. He left out the conversation with Trask. It was simple. He was asleep upstairs, the mics picked up the distinctive sound of the front door opening. No, the cameras were not yet working. He came downstairs in his underwear carrying his service weapon, saw a person behind the bar and started to approach with weapon ready. The person saw him and raised a pistol and Harp shot him twice. Nothing was said. Didn't know the guy. Wondered what he was doing. Found the bomb. Knew about these things. Looked for and found the detonator phone just to be sure. No land lines yet downstairs. Went back upstairs to call it in on his cell. Put on some clothes. Came back down and waited. End of story.

Carroll slowly shook his head and smiled. All his years as a policeman told him that there was more to this story. "So we got a known perp, a real badass, dead on the floor behind the bar with a gun in his hand in a place owned by one Horace B. Harper, known target of Mr. Arturo Donetti, which known seriously wounded target suddenly reappears as if from the dead after being gone for months. This known target of Mr. Donetti reappears at the same time as we find that, from all accounts, from a whole shitload of Federal and state agencies, Mr. Donetti has apparently disappeared."

Harp started to respond but Carroll held up his hand, "But wait, there's more. This perp, Mr. Donald Trask, a known mob enforcer employed by Mr. Donetti, is interrupted by Mr. Harper whilst placing a very powerful explosive on the premises now owned by Mr. Harper. And, lo and behold, Mr. Trask is shot dead by Mr. Harper."

Harp opened his mouth to speak, and again Carroll held up a hand. "Here's where the story gets to be real fun for those of us in law enforcement. While this same Mr. Harper is missing, a big, fancy estate hiding millions in cash up north of town, way out in the woods, is blown up and burned to the ground by unknown perp or perps, leaving money all over the place, some floating down a creek to the joy of landowners below. In the process of analyzing possible causes of this event, they find that two well-known bad dudes who might have been there are also missing and, being in the business they were in, assumed to be deceased or in Brazil, etc." Carroll continued, ignoring the activity as they removed Trask's body. Harp was listening intently, not because he didn't know what had happened but as a careful review of how well his tracks had been covered. "And then, I'm putting all this together as we speak, I get a call two days ago from this Pittsburg detective Joe Stephens who still carries a kind of grudge against you. He thinks you offed a guy at about 600 yards and got away with it up in some little Pennsylvania town way off in the boonies. Anyway, this Detective Stephens hears what's going on over here visa vi you. He calls and says to me, 'If known enemies Donetti and Harper both disappear for a long time, and then all of a sudden Harper reappears, then Donetti is dead and Harper did it. You can bet on it.'"

They sat in silence while both digested the meaning of all that Carroll had said. Harp concluded that the best thing he could say was nothing at all. Carroll concluded that he really didn't have anything to hold Harper on. Something was not right here, but the facts overrode these suspicions. Carroll's thoughts were interrupted by a patrolman who came back in to report that they had found Trask's car. It was easily found using the remote from Trask's pocket. It was the last piece of the night's puzzle. It was too simple. Trask drove to the neighborhood, walked to the bar, assumed the building was empty, picked the front door lock, was caught in the act of placing the bomb, and was killed by two pistol shots, one to the arm and one to the heart. Fingerprints substantiated the sequence of events. (Harp had left his prints on the bomb and cell phone, removed them from Trask's weapon, and placed Trask's prints back on it after his demise.)

Carroll announced the verdict. "Considering all the facts here, it looks like your actions were justified, Mr. Harper. For now, you are due the thanks of a grateful public for eliminating *another* real bad dude."

Harp caught the pointed implication of the word *another* but stayed silent.

"I'm curious about one thing, though. Aren't you worried that Arturo Donetti is still out there and will still try to get you?" He was watching Harp's response with sharp intensity.

Harp thought to himself that this guy was no fool. He would have to be very careful about his response to this particular topic now and in the future. "Sure. He could come back anytime. But I guess I'll just have to take my chances. I've got to live my life. I just hope the authorities get him first."

Carroll grinned. "Perfect answer. I would expect no less from our perfectly blameless Mr. Harper."

Carroll stood up and stretched. It was now close to 8 a.m. He had been up all night. "I'm going home to sleep for about twelve hours, then I'm going in to type up all my notes on this justifiable homicide." Carroll started for the door and paused, came back, and said, "Our medical guys did note one strange thing about this guy's wounds. The one in the shoulder had some slight blood coagulation. It seemed to have happened some time before the one to the heart. Maybe even several minutes before. You got any idea how that could happen?"

Harp shrugged and said, "Nope."

"Well, it doesn't change anything anyway. Just thought

you might have some thoughts on it." He smiled tiredly and turned to leave, then again, he stopped. "Oh, and you want to hear something else real funny about the Donetti connection? There was this little pasta place out on Dillman that was a secret meeting place for the Donetti enforcers. It was where they got paid. It was blown to pieces by high powered rifle shots while they were having one of their *secret* meetings. Turns out that the shots came from a little park maybe a quarter mile away as the crow flies. Even the SWAT guys say this was remarkable shooting. About forty rounds and none missed. Then, can you believe this?" Carroll shook his head and widened his eyes in mock wonder, "Some local cop coming back from a coffee stop practically stumbles over a package lying on the ground next to his patrol car. It even has a note. It said: *used at Dillman and Prother.* They run the ballistics and, sure enough, it was. Then they run the prints and, lo and behold, it belongs to a *Donetti* gunman! This guy is screaming all over the place that he didn't do it. Sounds convincing even. Doesn't matter. He is a bad dude, and we got him in custody on charges we haven't finished running up yet. Ain't that a scream?" Again, this very smart cop was intently watching Harp's response.

Harp just said, in carefully projected indifference, "I'm glad you got the guy."

Carroll appeared to be stifling a laugh. He waved at Harp and, with a sardonic grin, finally left. Harp sighed in relief. He, too, was very tired. He made sure the front door was closed and locked. Harp went back to bed thinking he was glad the Donetti thing was finally over.

It wasn't.

38

It was much worse this time. Again, the word spread rapidly. *Holy shit, this is the same guy who took out two mobsters!* They were all over the place. Harp quickly learned that he could not go anywhere near either the Battle or Vet LZ. He relented and gave one interview. He wanted to express his goal of creating a bar business designed mainly for service members and veterans, but when one intrepid reporter demanded to know why he enjoyed killing people so much, the interview was terminated. It was his first and last.

Fortunately, the media people hadn't yet found his condo, which had been purchased under the name of the limited liability company Kowalski had created to handle the money from the sale of the farm. Harp stayed there, regularly communicating with Tommy, Aaron, and Elliott by phone. This down time was different. He used it for two things: the work on the Vet LZ and ways he might spend the money taken from Donetti's vault. The strange thing was, he was not trying to keep this money. He wanted to get rid of it. He would gladly pay whatever the IRS demanded just for the freedom to put the money to good use. Most ironic was the fact that he just wanted to give it away and couldn't.

A tall chain link fence was thrown up all around the Vet LZ and work there continued. Concurrent work on the upstairs went as planned even though Harp could not imagine when he would be able to actually live there. The most expensive change was the expansion and design of the two unisex bathrooms in the bar to allow handicapped use. There would be chairless fixed tables along the wall opposite the bar especially suited for wheelchairs. Outside, on the lot to the right of the building, was a fenced pee and poop area for service dogs. It was fronted by a roofed smoking area the requisite twenty-five feet from the inside. Inside, toward the back of the bar room, was a small drinking and feeding area for service animals.

Harp knew he wasn't capable of going through the hiring process because he knew too little about the actual skills the business required. And, he wanted to hire veterans. Bonny had tended bar before, so Harp brought him in to do the hiring. Bonny put together a staff of dedicated veterans who wanted the concept to work. Having Bonny do it also accomplished another important step in the operation. Bonny had fought beside the owner and knew him very well. He could explain Harp and Harp's goals in running the establishment. There were no gender barriers. A female veteran held the same status as a male. All branches were equal. There was a sign at the front door that very emphatically demanded that all who entered must show respect for everyone. Another big sign on the back bar said *If you can't hold it, don't drink it.* Patrons who could not hold it were warned once, then barred for a month. All rules were enforced by a small cadre of staffers who were afraid of nothing. And, of course, there was a rule that unlicensed weapons were not allowed.

The Vet LZ was a hit from the first day. It was designed to

meet any special needs of veterans, but anyone who followed the rules was welcome. As human nature dictates, however, it would soon be obvious to any non-veteran who came in on a busy day that he or she was somehow different from the rest of the patrons. As with most public establishments, the sense of being welcome was most important to new patrons. Most new patrons were hesitant when first entering, but the bartender would tell them to come on in and say the first drink is on the house. There were always camo and other military gear evident, but most people came in civvies.

When the interest in his personal affairs died down, Harp moved into the upstairs apartment. He would come down through the kitchen and have his usual drinks at the bar. He invoked an owner's prerogative, however, and had a table of his own in the shadows against the back wall. On busy nights, he would sit at his table and watch with pleasure as customers enjoyed their visits to his business. He was not unapproachable, but it soon became clear that he preferred to remain alone. This became part of the SOP (Standard Operating Procedure) for the Vet LZ.

That's where he was sitting, doing paperwork, which he despised, when he saw the man enter. He was a tall slender figure wearing fatigues like he was comfortable in them. He wore military issue aviator eyeglasses over a pleasant and mostly forgettable face. He removed his hat and walked over to the bartender with a question. The bartender pointed at Harp. The man nodded and approached. From experience Harp first noticed the eagles on the man's collars. A Colonel. Then he recognized the face. Harp closed his eyes and slowly shook his head and mumbled, "Shit." It was the guy from the whatever-the-hell-it-was government agency who had figured out Harp's actions that ended up with him burying two spooks somewhere out West. The guy had promised a kind of immunity then, but here he was. It couldn't be good.

Harp remained seated even though his first inclination was to leap to his feet and salute. The Colonel walked up to the table. "Mind if I sit down, Sergeant Harper?"

Harp motioned toward a chair and waited.

The Colonel sat, smiled, and waved a hand around indicating the entire establishment. "This place is really impressive. We've heard about it, and I've been looking forward to seeing it in person. You've done a good job building this business."

"You know my name, but I don't know yours," Harp hinted.

"Smith," The Colonel replied with a slight smile.

Harp knew that was bullshit but offered, "You like a drink, Colonel *Smith*?"

"Nah, I'm working." He put his hat on the table and pulled a plastic envelope from his shirt pocket.

Harp had a sense of déjà vu. He had been there before, and that time it had been a hoax.

Smith sighed and laid an arm on the table. The envelope was in the other hand. "God, I am tired. Just got in and they give me this." He held up the envelope. It held a small spent brass cartridge. "Did you know that the FBI will try to convict on as few as 7 matching points from a finger print?" He was watching Harp. Harp felt safe. He had been careful. It wasn't his. "Usually, the courts want at least 10 or 12 points for a conviction." He held up the envelope. "There are just 7 matching points on this nine-millimeter cartridge. But, you know what? The computer thought it was enough to kick out the thumb print on one Senior Master Sergeant Horace B. Harper."

Harp waited. He was stunned. He could not think where he had fucked up.

Smith slid to the edge of the chair and slumped, with his hands interlaced across his chest and ankles crossed. He was watching bar patrons as he went on in a conversational tone. "You may not be aware that there was an attack on a secret hide-away of one bad boy Arturo Donetti way out in the woods of New Jersey a few weeks ago. The nature of the attack and its results ended up involving just about every damned law enforcement agency in the country. I mean, hell, there was money, drugs, explosives, the mob—there was something there for everybody."

The Colonel now sat up and turned to face Harp. "Everybody but the Army, that is. But some smart little First Lieutenant in our office, that gets to see everything, everywhere, by the way, noticed that this had the earmarks of a military operation. The timing, the method, the materials, the execution, all pointed toward military experience. You know what they did? Just for the hell of it, they sent a little team out to study it as a military operation, a kind of training exercise. Totally on the QT of course. In working it out, our boys said that there had to be a vantage point from which the perpetrator could operate. They found this large tree way up the far bank across this deep ravine. And, yup, there were boot marks, scuff marks, and with a little metal detecting, one spent nine-millimeter cartridge on that little level spot behind that tree."

Then Harp remembered. He found all but one spent cartridge. Smith continued, "Then of course there were these boot tracks going from this spot down to the creek. That's where they were completely obliterated by all the activity around that room full of cash. For all we know, this person, who has a thumbprint very similar to yours, carried away a bunch of cash." Smith turned again to face Harp. "Then, of course, it is logical to pursue the existence of a spent cartridge and its place with relation to the overall mission. If there were shots fired, who or what was the target?" Smith smiled. "And, knowing our Sergeant Harper as we do, we know that he hits what he shoots at. What would he be shooting at? Maybe we should dig a little deeper."

Harp cringed at the word *dig*. It took every bit of control Harp could muster to keep a straight face. He even managed a casual shrug. "It sounds like a whole lot of supposition to me. What do you want, Colonel Smith?"

"Not much, really. Our people tend to think your 'thumb' was there, which would mean you did the dirty deed." He shifted in the chair and continued, "But seven matching points is simply not enough to convict. It would be like identifying a person's face when all you could see was the corner of an eye along with a small part of the cheek. Now, a mother might be able to do it with her child, and an overlay might match perfectly, but it isn't incontrovertible evidence. Theoretically, another match would be possible."

It went totally against his own moral code but Harp lied. "Your *people* are wrong. I wasn't anywhere near this place, wherever it is. Besides, I would have been too weak from my wounds to do anything like that."

Smith slapped his leg, startling Harp. "That's exactly what I wanted to hear!" He stood up. "I will relay this information to our boys and we'll get this line of thinking shut down post haste." He picked up his hat, looked down at Harp who was still sitting, too stunned to move. "You are doing a good job here with this place. Keep it up." Then, more philosophically, he observed, "Everyone has secrets, Sergeant Harper. That's our business. Smart people keep 'em. Others don't and others die." Harp, who was still sitting, was slightly chilled at the underlying meaning of those words. Smith added, "You know what keeps us so interested in you, Sergeant Harper? We keep wondering—who's next?" Smith strolled through the bar to the front door, nodding and smiling to the people. Harp noted that the damned spent shell with his thumb print went with him. What the hell did that mean?

EPILOGUE

It was a busy night and the Vet LZ was hopping. As the fates decree, several things happened at roughly the same time. The bartender broke a wine glass and, in the process, got a deep cut in the palm of his hand. It would require stitches, so he was rushed out the door to a nearby clinic. The backup bartender was out of town and the waiter had anxiety issues and adamantly refused to get behind the bar. Harp was it. Harp began serving drinks but was soon totally jammed. He was pouring triples and spilling singles in the process. He could not get the cash register to work, so he just left the drawer open and made change by rounding up or down to the nearest dollar. Normally, Harp was not the kind of guy to get flustered. He had been in battle with the responsibility to remain cool and make good decisions or people would die, but serving drinks to thirty or forty thirsty people at the same time brought him to the point of meltdown. He was one red-faced, cross, sweaty, flustered bartender.

It was right at the point where he was just about ready to tell everybody to get their own damn drinks when Kowalski walked in. There was a sudden silence in the establishment that Harp would have noted if he hadn't been so overwhelmed. The tall, gorgeous, impeccably dressed and coifed woman strode through the crowd of mostly men as only Attorney Sandra Kowalski could do it. Harp was bent over the sink, trying to wash at least two or three glasses. He had been serving drinks in dirty glasses thinking what the hell, it's alcohol, it kills germs. Kowalski came to the spot at the bar opposite where Harp was working and cussing. She started laughing. That familiar sound brought his head up. And, as usual with their stormy relationship, and with a mean scowl, he responded poorly. "What the hell's so funny?"

Kowalski also responded poorly and, with smile gone and flat angry lips, turned and walked back toward the door. An awareness of his own stupidity suddenly hit Harp, but she was almost at the door. Harp did the only thing he could think of: "Stop that woman!" he shouted as loud as he could. Immediately five large men came to their feet and blocked passage to the door. There was silence in the room. The evening had all of a sudden become very interesting. Kowalski stood facing this blockade with her back to Harp. Everyone waited to see what came next.

Without thinking, Harp continued giving orders. "Tell her I'm sorry." Kowalski did nothing. A woman with a large burn mark on the left side of her face at a table next to where Kowalski was standing rose from her chair and faced Kowalski. In a quiet voice, she said, "He's really sorry or he wouldn't be saying this in front of all of us. You should go back."

Kowalski replied, talking to the woman, "Why should I? Maybe you don't know it, but he's a total asshole."

"Yeah, but he's a good asshole. He's done a lot for us, for me. Go back and at least talk. Please?"

But still Kowalski stood facing the door. Five large men still stood blocking the way. Finally, Harp got the words out, but like he was still shouting orders. "Tell her I need her. Tell her I miss her."

At this, Kowalski's shoulders slumped. She had wanted to hear those words. She dreaded hearing those words. Of all the people in this world, this was the one who drove her nuts. This was the one she wanted to be with. She even dreamed about him. Why him?

The woman very gently put her hands on Kowalski's shoulders and turned her back toward Harp. Harp came from behind the bar and, in an imploring voice that he had used maybe twice in his entire life said, "Come back...*please*." The last time was when, as a young boy, he was begging his mother to stop drinking. She didn't and she died.

Kowalski paused. She looked at the woman with hands on her shoulders and mouthed a thanks then gently patted a scarred hand. It had turned into a sort of play, a drama, where the patrons became a totally engaged audience. There now was complete silence. They felt they knew Harp. He was one of them. They did not know this beautiful woman, but anyone could see that they cared about each other.

The path from Harp to Kowalski through the crowd was a lane that was clear of people but full of portent. Harp waited, knowing there was a lot more on the line than a simple walk back to the bar. It was time for him to either light the fuse or pull the plug. He knew in his heart which it would be.

Kowalski was thinking the same thing. If I walk back to this guy, I'll never to be able to walk away again. She knew in her heart which it would be. Kowalski shook herself as if to recover, then walked steadily to stand nose to nose with Harp to declare,

"I am a lawyer, a damned good lawyer. I will always be a lawyer no matter what the hell we do, no matter what kind of idiot decisions you make."

Harp put his hands on her shoulders, looked into her eyes and declared, "You can do whatever you want to do, however you want to do it, and I will support you with all my heart no matter what—as long as you come back to me." Harp wrapped his arms around her and she responded doing the same with him. Each held the other in a sort of relief that these volatile feelings they had felt toward each other for years had somehow survived. The crowd whistled and cheered.

When they parted, Harp asked in desperation, "Do you know how to fix drinks?"

Kowalski scoffed. "How do you think I worked my way through law school? Gimme an apron." She hung her coat on the rack at the end of the bar.

Harp leaned in close and whispered, "If somebody can't pay, it's free." She nodded and smiled at Harp.

Kowalski tied the apron high up under her breasts and took over the operation. The attention of the patrons was immediate. First, in her strong courtroom voice, she ordered everyone to listen up. Then she turned and drew a line with her hand along a shelf on the back bar and announced, "Everything above this line is ten dollars. Everything else is five dollars. No frozen drinks." She raised both hands, pointing at the row of smiling faces and asked, "Who's next?"

Acknowledgements

To write and publish a book is a complex and challenging endeavor. I am certain that, if I were alone in this creative process, I would never make it through all the steps one must take before it gets to the printer. There were many friends and family members who were pushing, pulling, and prodding to get me over the finish line. Chief among those is my wife, Mary, who, most fortunate for me, is smart, talented, and determined. I leaned heavily on a small set of readers who dug deeply into the manuscript and found that I am nowhere near as grammatically capable as I thought. My dear brother-in-law, Dr. Robert G. Stephens, III, found the time in a busy life to provide a deep and careful analysis. My old friend Richard Peckham also volunteered his valuable time to take it apart so we could put it back together. My son Jefferson, though a Geologist, showed a great talent for finding those insidious errors that had been missed by all others. And, finally, I want to thank Bob Babcock, CEO of Deeds Publishing, an old soldier who has been very supportive in my efforts with this and previous books.

About the Author

D.E. Hopper is a family man and veteran who enjoys the extreme good fortune of having a loving wife and two smart, healthy sons. Using the wonderful G.I. Bill, he worked his way through three college degrees. He remains especially proud of having served his country at many locations around the world during a four-year stint in the Air Force Strategic Command, mainly in a Reconnaissance Wing. He is reasonably literate with experience in technical writing, editing, and writing for personal pleasure. *Who's Next* is the sequel to his first novel, *Shot by Harp*. He is also the author of *Words Will*, a book of prose and poems.

CPSIA information can be obtained
at www.ICGtesting.com
Printed in the USA
FSHW011644111120
75676FS